ALLAN CAMERON was born in 195: East Pakistan (later Bangladesh). H< his education. He worked at sea an he lived for many years. The trad< mastered include postman, labourer, factory worker, forwarding clerk, hydrographic surveyor and university lecturer. For the last ten years he has finally settled down on the Isle of Lewis, where he writes and translates.

His first novel, *The Golden Menagerie*, was published by Luath Press in May 2004. He has written for the daily newspaper *L'Unità*, the Italian current affairs magazine *Reset*, and the academic journals *Teoria Politica* and *Renaissance Studies*. He has translated some twenty books by a variety of writers, including the Italian philosopher Norberto Bobbio, the president of the European Commission Romano Prodi, and the leading historian Eric Hobsbawm.

The Berlusconi Bonus

ALLAN CAMERON

Luath Press Limited

EDINBURGH

www.luath.co.uk

Quoted material from *Europe: A History* by Norman Davies is
reproduced by permission of Oxford University Press.

First published 2005

The paper used in this book is recyclable.
It is made from low-chlorine pulps produced in a low-energy,
low-emission manner from renewable forests.

Printed and bound by
DigiSource GB Ltd, Livingston

Typeset in 11 point Sabon

For all historians who exchange our dangerous and divisive myths for complex and often incomprehensible truths that unite us in their confusion.

And with apologies to Francis Fukuyama whose ideas I satirise not because he is their worst exponent but because he is their best (moreover I do not mention that he has more recently slackened the brake on history that he so deftly operates).

The First Draft of Adolphus Hibbert's Confession

The First Draft of Adolphus Hibbert's Confession

HISTORY HAS RESTARTED, and our Glorious Revolution is driving it forward. We in the Military Records Department are making our essential contribution to the betterment of mankind and are working our way through the archives of the previous degenerate regime. This is a colossal task and one fitting of our Benign Regime and our Great Helmsman. Much of the material coming out of the notorious Central Surveillance Agency is frankly rather banal, but I was recently passed this strange confession, which is not really a confession at all but an excellent account of how things really were during the oppressive 'End-of-History' Age. It reveals the cruel and mischievous nature of the previous capitalist regime, which is personified by the nefarious figure of Captain Hieronymus Younce who sadly was able to die in his bed at an advanced age, after having spent his retirement in the cultivation of an unusual hybrid of rose.

Younce demanded a confession from a rather silly adventurer and anti-social element called Adolphus Hibbert, and this is the first draft. At the time, prisoners were required to keep submitting confessions until the authorities found them acceptable. Recalcitrant elements were tortured. The system was effective because early drafts provided the information and later ones provided obeisance to the regime. We know very little about what happened to Hibbert after he finally submitted an acceptable confession, some three years and thirty-five attempts later. The confessions, as was normal, became shorter and shorter, and of course increasingly submissive. We do know that his Berlusconi Bonus was withdrawn shortly after his arrest in 2052 and that he died in a mental hospital in 2076. His medical records show he suffered from an increasingly delusional state and his doctors never showed the slightest inclination to certify him ready for reintegration into normal society.

At first I was minded to release this unusual work for the edification of all the masses, but it then occurred to me that the writer had a dangerously petty-bourgeois and anarchoid frame of mind that could be contagious and deleterious to our Glorious Revolution. We too have to protect the secrecy of our Benign Regime from the prying eyes of subversives and defeatists. It is not so much Younce's methods that I object to (indeed they are very instructive), but the regime he served. I have therefore decided that in order to avoid possible misinterpretations by persons of unsound mind, this book is not appropriate for general release, and I have restricted its circulation to members of the Inner Party, pending the final decision of the Office of the Great Helmsman.

Captain Archibald Truman
CenSurvMassCon
Great Helmsmanville, 2084

CHAPTER ONE

The Explosion

WHAT CAN I say? They tell me that if I want to get out of here I must first tell my story – confess my sins, as it were. I have to bare my soul. I have to let them inspect and probe the workings of my mind – my poor, confused and rebellious mind. Only then will they decide whether I am ready to be returned to society. I have to start at the beginning, they say, but when I ask them when that was, they are evasive, perhaps even irritated by my inability to make this project mine. They probably want me to start with my tender years and a whole lot of autobiographical crap – psychobabble about why mistreatment as a child led to criminal and antisocial behaviour. That stuff lets both them and me off the hook. Everyone's a winner. Isn't that meant to be the secret of our wonderful consumer civilisation?

They are so powerful, so incredibly powerful with their shining building, their heavy steps on the corridors, their busyness and above all the secrecy of their purpose. I never know what they are going to do next, but I know there must be a purpose to their seemingly irrational and erratic behaviour. It is true that they leave me alone to write, so they can better judge the sincerity of my confession, but the noise of their bustle and their sudden entrances into my cell seem to clutter my mind and leave me little room to think. This confession should be a way of letting me think about what I have done, about all those who have suffered because of what I have done and about why I should feel guilty and why I should not. That old chestnut – the oldest of chestnuts: do I regret anything? Would I just do it all over again? Did I corrupt or was I corrupted? And so on.

I think I'll start with when I went to register for the Berlusconi Bonus. It seems as good a place as any. I went along the Sunny-Virgin Line and changed at Victoria for the Glaxon-Curtiss Best-Deal Line. I got out at Holborn. A cold wind chilled an empty platform, and that emptiness accentuated the shabbiness of the station: the cracked tiles, the slime on the walls, the corners of the advertising posters flapping endlessly, pointlessly, and the heavy clank-clank of the ageing machinery that drove the escalator. My appointment was with a lawyer called Spartacus Linklater who I had engaged to carry out the registration. On the escalator I looked at the adverts for products no longer sold – for products once sold in massive quantities to the busy human stream that used to flow in both directions through the station. Now these relics from the past marked the passing years by fading into a melancholy grey. At the top of the escalator as I entered the area where the through-draught is strongest and coldest, I met a man I later came to know as Captain Younce. He was an athletic and well-dressed man with dark hair, bushy eyebrows and a prominent chin. He smiled and walked straight up to me.

'Mr Adolphus Hibbert?'

'Yes,' I said, taken aback. 'And who are you?'

'A great admirer of your business acumen. I hear that you are after a BB.'

'And what if I am? Is it any of your business?'

'Everybody's business is my business. But don't be alarmed. I have to know everything about you, and I can safely say that I have found nothing, absolutely nothing in your past life that could possibly disqualify you from a Berlusconi Bonus.'

It seemed that Linklater had given me away. So much for professional confidentiality. This policeman or whoever he was could investigate my business and land me with a ruinous tax bill or possibly a prison sentence. I was so close to safety and yet this man could take it all away from me.

He smiled the smile of a man who knows he is in control and is alone in understanding the encounter. 'I've told you not to worry. We've all committed the odd misdemeanour, the odd tax fiddle, the slightly fraudulent deal. That is capitalism. That is the free market. We'll be very happy to see you amongst those who hold the reigns of power.' He paused with the self-ironic smirk that announces a forthcoming platitude, clapped me on the back with inappropriate familiarity and said, 'That is the name of the game'.

Naturally I was embarrassed and irritated by this meeting. I had done things I wasn't particularly proud of, and the idea that someone might know my private affairs came as a shock. Without looking him in the face and terrified of his power, his unknown power delegated by an unknown authority, I told him I had an appointment and excused myself. As I attempted to leave, he held my arm in a steel grip: 'When you get your Berlusconi Bonus you will be above the law of the land, but you will not be above our law.'

'Your law?'

'Yes the law of the Central Surveillance Agency. With a BB, you pay no tax, you can bribe whoever you wish, your right to fraudulent business practice goes without saying, you can murder almost with impunity, and you can even rape women and bugger boys as long as they or their parents don't have BBs as well. But you cannot endanger the security of the state.'

'Why would I want to do that?'

'Why indeed? It is precisely because such a thought would never go through your brain that I am so happy to let you go ahead and get your Berlusconi Bonus, but I always like to warn candidates that there are limits to what you can do with a BB. There is a higher authority that supervises it all, that looks after you, your Berlusconi Bonus and the whole system which is so beneficial to us all.'

'But I thought that with the advent of the Free Market we had reduced the powers of the state.'

'The interfering state. We did away with the interfering state, the nanny state that looks after those whom nature never intended to succeed, but even a non-interventionist state has to defend itself against subversion. You follow my drift?'

To be honest, I understood very little of what he was trying to say. I was a businessman. I got on with the job of making money and creating wealth. I thought all that politics stuff was in the past. Of course there were the Al-Qaeda terrorists and their outrages, but you were never sure what they wanted and who they were trying to hit. It was unpleasant, but you got on with your life. That's what I thought then. That was my world, and I felt very secure in it. The way we live seemed appropriate and even natural.

He let go of my arm, and annoyingly he clapped me on the back again with his other hand and wished me luck with the BB. He turned and went, leaving me paralysed by the suddenness of the whole encounter and its obscure meanings. I pulled myself together and set off for Linklater's office.

By the time I got there, I was angry – I was boiling. 'Where's Linklater?' I shouted at the secretary and carried straight on into his study. There was a client in there: an undernourished and inconsequential man with spectacles and one of those thin moustaches that run along the ridge of the upper lip. He seemed so stunned that he momentarily drew my attention away from Linklater and slightly slowed the momentum of my anger. 'What have you been telling the police, Linklater? How can they know about my BB application? I thought lawyers were meant to respect customer confidentiality.'

Linklater came round the desk in a second, and with a strained face right up close to mine, he whispered in a harsh, urgent voice, 'You fool, Adolphus, do you think this application is like getting a driving licence? These people knew about your intentions before I did; even before you did, probably. You could get yourself into a lot of trouble shouting about a BB application.'

As this sobered me, he turned and in a normal voice asked the man to leave and make another appointment. The man scuttled out with a backward glance at me that revealed both anger and envy.

Once the door had closed, Linklater returned to his desk, stretched himself and looked at me with a nod of disapproval. 'You're getting a BB, for Christ's sake. Do you know what that means? It means you can do anything you like. They don't hand them out like confetti. I live well but I couldn't dream of a BB. Not in a thousand years. I'm a lawyer in a very litigious society, but I could never earn like you. You sell drugs and equipment to the Free Market Super-Saver Trust Hospitals. That's got to be the best way of making money these days. In fact the only people making the real bucks seem to be those who supply privatised companies subsidised by the government. And you practically throw it away with your big mouth. Just as well that idiot you just saw is not the type to blackmail you while the application goes through.'

'How long?' I asked imperiously, but I felt hot and stupid – an unpleasant internal sensation that manifested itself through a rush of warmth to my face and an equally unpleasant external sensation of prickly sweat. It was impossible to gauge how much of this confusion was visible to Linklater. 'How long will it take?'

Linklater seemed a cold fish, but was known as a reliable lawyer. He liked to take his time and was obsessive about providing his customers with the best legal opinion. 'Well, it could be a month, it could be six months or it could be more than a year. They may turn you down, and there is no appeal. Then you'll have the Fraud Squad and the Inland Revenue crawling all over your properties. It depends how much they like you and whether they want you in their club. The Berlusconi Bonus is officially called a Plutocratic Social Gratitude Award, and is supposed to reward the extremely rich for all the wealth they give back to society through the so-called trickle-down effect, but the newspapers, with their love of alliterations, quickly named it after some European prime minister who lived when there was history. It appears that some people had accused him of altering the laws to get himself out of some legal difficulties. With the rise of plutocracy, the rich decided that they should formalise this reality and introduce a set of legally recognised privileges that are triggered at a certain level of wealth which, as you know, now stands at 1.2 billion dollars. Everybody knows the Berlusconi Bonus exists, but for many years the newspapers have been loathe to mention it. It is a strange world we live in.'

'In what way?'

There was something professorial about Linklater, with his tall gangling body, stooped back and unfashionable glasses. At the time I thought him an oddball but I later understood that his constant reading had separated him from the rest of us, and created the kind of eccentric thinking that made him puzzle over my entirely reasonable question. 'Well, this thing about history, for a start.' I saw him suppress his desire to speak, and I believe this took a great effort on his part. He looked pensive and irritated. He stared at me for some time and mused, 'Strange times indeed.' He immediately got down to business, produced the prepared documents for signing and then sent me on my way with the promise that he would contact me as soon as the Berlusconi Bonus had been issued.

When I left Linklater's office, I went down Holborn and turned right into the Strand. I felt elated but also inexplicably nervous. I was close to the realisation of my dreams, and yet I was already aware that they would involve realities I had never expected. There was that strange official I met at the tube station, and the expression of the man in the lawyer's office, which appeared to be envy but also expressed the fact that soon I would be a man like very few others, a man of privilege and power. I sensed that power would also involve isolation and dangers I was not yet aware of.

Walking with no particular purpose, I came into Thatcher Square. It is impressively large and surrounded by fine buildings erected during the history period. In the centre there is an enormous column and at the top there is the statue of a middle-aged woman with a handbag. She is Thatcher, an important politician who also lived when there was history and did much to further the free market from which society is supposed to benefit so much. It was during election time and there was a large crowd listening to a politician from the New Freedom Party. Personally, I have never bothered to vote. When I was working so hard to get rich and obtain my Berlusconi Bonus, I never concerned myself with politics. In my holiday mood however, I was drawn by the spectacle, the music, the colours of the bunting, the hysterical excitement of the crowd and the politician's ritual slogans and rhetorical questions. 'The New Liberty Party is trying to smear me and smear my party. Why? Because they don't want to talk about the issues'. The crowd erupted in praise and shook with an irrational enthusiasm. 'And what are the issues? The issues are education, health and above all security.' Again the crowd transformed into a troublingly ecstatic state, as though the man's words were completely unexpected. 'Yes, and we are going to deliver. Do you hear? We are going to deliver on education, health and above all security.' The crowd responded in its typical fashion, as though it had been turned on by an unseen electric wire.

I moved to the outer edge of the crowd, fascinated but also slightly unnerved. 'Isn't he great?' said a smartly dressed young woman with an expectation of agreement. Embarrassed I moved along the outer perimeter of that island of bodies. As I distanced myself from her, I turned and saw that she was following me with a perplexed expression. In that instant something lit up from behind her, a ball of light or fire, and noise that was so loud it sounded faint and hit me with a physical weight that lifted me up and threw me to the ground. For a moment afterwards there was silence. The part of the crowd that had not been damaged by the bomb swayed in disbelief. Then from the chaos of bodies and blood, the first cries and screams lifted up in anger, shock and already a desire for explanations.

The police and ambulances were immediately there. They appeared to have no questions or disbelief. It all appeared to be for them a natural and highly predictable event. The dead and injured were cleared with a speed that seemed almost as instantaneous as the bomb itself – that challenged our own memories of the horror and our ability to retain them. Those of us who were closest to the blast were rounded up by the police. You would think from the way they treated us that we were the perpetrators of the outrage. I found myself next to the woman who had spoken to me so emphatically. Her clothes were blackened down her back and her face was scratched from being thrown to the ground. 'What are they going to do to us?' she cried, grabbing my arm and staring into my face in search of an answer.

'Why should they do anything to us?' I asked.

'We witnessed an event,' she replied in a strained voice.
'So?'
'If you put a lot of events together you get history.'
For the second time in that extraordinary day I had heard the word 'history', not the kind of thing we are supposed to discuss, but I suppose that we are all more or less aware of it and puzzled by its taboo.

'They will want to question us so that they can get some clues. Clues that could lead to the arrest of the terrorists,' I tried to reassure her, but from the look on her face I am not certain that I succeeded. At that moment, I noticed two men in suits were talking to the police. They reminded me of the official I had met at the tube station earlier. They were confident, well-built men with sharp features and short, neatly coiffured hair. They spoke with obvious authority and then one of them pointed to me. The policemen entered the circle of two hundred or so witnesses and made their way towards me by pushing aside these shocked and frightened individuals. Many of them were suffering from minor cuts and bruises, but they seemed unconcerned and more focused on the possible dangers of their situation.

'Excuse me, sir, but would you like to step this way,' one of the policemen asked as he grabbed me by the arm and directed me out of the group of witnesses. 'You are free to go,' he announced with a slightly condescending air. 'Remember, sir, that there are many dangers in moving around the city. You will recall, I'm sure, the words of our president: since the end of history, society has become so developed that you can consume to your heart's content without ever leaving the confines of your home.'

CHAPTER TWO

The Intruder

ON RETURNING TO my home in Hampstead, I found another surprise awaited me in the form of Captain Younce. I opened the three burglar-proof locks and entered the hall. The mechanical secretary was switched off but the hall and sitting-room lights were turned on. There was an unnatural air about the place, as though everything had been tampered with and put back exactly where it was, but my mind was picking up miniscule alterations in their positions and orientations. I entered the sitting room immediately to find the captain seated in the armchair and very much at home. He stood up slowly and this time introduced himself.

'Very sorry to hear about what happened this afternoon in Thatcher Square. You have to be careful when you go out these days, if you'll excuse the expression.'

Captain Younce could be very pleasant if he wanted to. You felt that he was not a man to be crossed lightly, but he had a good manner when he wanted – or when he wanted something. I said nothing and smiled weakly. He smiled back. 'First the good news. We have decided to grant you the Berlusconi Bonus. The letter is already in the post and on its way to your lawyer.'

'Oh, thank you,' I replied, genuinely moved and grateful. My status was assured.

'Think nothing of it, my man. You are ideal for this honour. You have a proven track record of producing wealth and you deserve some protection from the state.'

'Thank you, Captain. Thank you,' I grovelled.

'There is something you could do for me.'

'Really?'

'To start with I would like to know what Linklater discussed with you today.' I mentioned my entrance and the misunderstanding with a little concern, but at the time it would never have occurred to me to lie to Younce. He wasn't interested in any of our business dealings, but asked me what I thought of Linklater as a man.

'Well, everyone speaks very highly of his knowledge of the law,' I said vaguely.

'Typical of a man obsessed with the history period! A primitive type who should have lived in more primitive times,' Younce pronounced with the certitude of someone who has long ago made up his mind on the argument. 'Knowledge of the law is of no importance now. You pay for your course and you pay for your degree. Study is no longer a productive activity aimed at reaching an end, but a consumer good to be purchased. It is not the cleverness of your lawyer that makes the difference, but the hourly rate he charges. The more he charges the more likely it is that you will achieve the desired result. Typical of the man. His wrong-headedness never ceases to astound me. He really doesn't know how to enjoy himself. That's the root of the problem. He has the kind of puritanical streak that inhibits the natural hedonism of human beings, the hedonism that has been perfected by the Rational Consumer Implant Card.' Younce paused to give weight to the perversity of it all. 'Did Linklater mention anything unusual?'

'Nothing in particular. He did mention history. I distinctly remember a mention of history.'

'Did he now?' said the captain leaning forward, and his eyes lit up with interest. 'Did he now? We could have him just for that. But I would prefer you to get a little more information out of him first.'

'Me?'

'Yes, you would be ideal. Reliable, accepting of society's fundamental values, and not generally interested in politics. You are ideal.'

'What do you want me to do?'

'Here are two tickets to a Fukuyama End-Of-History Theme Park. Linklater appears to have a particular weakness for these theme parks. Now, I wouldn't want you to mention today's terrorist attack to anyone, but in the case of Linklater I'll make an exception. He'll take it as a sign of trust: he may open up a bit. Linklater is at the centre of a group of subversives, a particularly dangerous group that could constitute a real problem if not handled properly. We wouldn't want history to start again, would we? Because that's what these people would like to do.'

'I cannot understand why,' I engaged with conformist zeal. 'We know that the human condition was terrible at the time of history: the appalling quality of life, the nonexistent standard of living and the complete lack of consumer choice. We think of it as quaint, but in reality it must have been rather tedious.'

'Exactly. Well put. It must have been tedious indeed. History was tedious, so we had it banned.'

'Thus banning tedium.'

'Exactly! I like you, Hibbert, you've got a good head on your shoulders. You're not the sort to have your mind turned by a bunch of subversives.'

'And why are they letting off bombs and killing innocent people?' I asked. 'If Linklater is mixed up in that kind of thing, then I would look on it as my duty.'

'Steady now. Remember the rational self-interest on which our society is based. We will of course make it worth your while, and given the fact that you are already an extremely rich young man, we will have to pay you handsomely for your time in terms of both money and influence. I should add that the latter is much more important: it brings in even more money and is also so enjoyable.' Younce stopped to savour one of his moments of reflection and then added, 'Linklater is a strange fish. He's a romantic in a way. But he's right up to his neck in it.'

'And you want me to provide you with evidence so that you can arrest him.'

'Good God no. We live in an era in which there is the rule of men and not the rule of laws. I'll arrest him whenever I like, but I need more information. Information is more important than bodies. Anyone can pick up bodies. That's work for the police. I deal with finer, more complex matters. Christ man, you should know; you've just got yourself a Berlusconi Bonus. If that's not putting someone above the law, I'd like to know what is. But that doesn't mean that there aren't procedures that have to be strictly adhered to. The trouble with people like Linklater is that it is impossible to discuss them without getting into areas that are... well, that are frankly taboo at the moment. I've just used the word "era". I've thrown people in prison for ten years for less than that.'

'So I invite him to the theme park, tell him about the bomb and enter into his confidence. What else do I have to do?'

'Just observe and report. I ask no more.'

CHAPTER THREE

The Fukuyama End-Of-History Theme Park

I HAVE TO CONFESS that, on my way to Linklater's office for our second meeting, I was subject to a kind of euphoria or rather euphoric sense of being a principal actor in events of great importance – to whom I was not sure – to the Federation of Free Democratic States, perhaps, or to the defence of our freedoms. So much had happened. I was about to become one of the powerful in a plutocratic society that gives all its prizes to those who are already rich. And then there was this business of spying for the Central Surveillance Agency. I had seen many spy movies from the age of history and as I made my way up the Strand, I felt a sense of power, importance and physical well-being which also translated into a heightened sexual desire. For many years I had let my ambitions suppress my pleasures, but now I would be free to enjoy them in the sureness of no financial cost. My money would look after itself.

Of course, in the age of history their city streets were full of people, while ours are almost empty, desolate places. This gives them a kind of melancholy beauty and a fascinating redundancy in a period in which most things are so new, so plastic and so brightly coloured. I had come to live in the city partly out of a need to avoid people, but now I wanted people around me. I wanted to display my wealth, my strength, my power, my new more assertive step and posture. I assuaged these impulses merely by making a mental note to buy a really good suit. Looking back, I am both amused by and ashamed of my arrogance and stupidity. I had no idea of what I was getting into: the CSA does not seem a serious threat in our society and does not figure greatly in the lives of ordinary citizens. But this simply demonstrates the sophistication of its methods. This is the sign of a secret service that really knows its business.

Linklater was at his desk, eyes blinking at a world that was not his. You always had the impression that the world of books was more real to him than our world of buying and selling – he seemed to have contempt for the very thing that distinguishes human beings from the animals, namely the exchange of goods in a free market. I did not envy his other-worldliness at the time, although I later came to respect, and indeed envy, his erudition.

He looked at me with distaste and assumed a false congratulatory tone. 'You must have friends in high places? I have never heard of a BB application going through so quickly in all the years I have been practising law.'

He had me sign off the papers and his brusque manners implied that he wanted me out of the office as soon as possible. His hand trembled slightly. His frostiness presented me with a problem: new as I was to the spy business, I did not know how to invite him to the Fukuyama. I had to reopen a dialogue with a man who usually spoke too much about incomprehensible things, but had chosen that day to be taciturn.

'I was interested in what you were saying about history the other day,' was my opening gambit.

'Really? I have no memory of such a conversation. I'm sure it was tiresome.'

'No, it was fascinating. You don't hear much about history these days.'

'Indeed it is against the law, so we had better not compound any previous illegal activities by talking about it again.'

'Well actually I am very interested in history.'

'Is that so?' said Linklater with a sarcastic smile.

I wanted to succeed, not least because I wanted to please Younce. He was, after all, responsible for fast-tracking my BB application. We are strange animals: such a mixture of cynicism and naivety. We can lie and cheat, and then attribute the most absurdly benign motives to others, if those others command respect. It was obvious to the meanest intelligence that Captain Hieronymus Younce did not speed up the process because he particularly liked me or cared about my welfare, in spite of all his backslapping. He did it for his own professional reasons, and yet I wanted to believe that this complete stranger had done me a personal favour, and that I owed him something. I remembered that he had given me permission to mention the bomb incident to Linklater. He must have believed that this could have opened up our adversary. 'I was present when a bomb exploded in Thatcher Square yesterday,' I said artlessly, and waited for a reaction.

Linklater slowly lifted his eyes to look at me. 'Many casualties?' he asked.

'Yes,' I replied tersely – lacking as I did any concept of what he might be thinking but nevertheless aware of the concern in his voice.

He shook his head and a bitter tiredness descended on him. 'You seem to be everywhere, Mr Hibbert, and no one minds that you know so many things.' He spoke as though I were both powerful, thus requiring a defensive stance, and odious, thus requiring his contempt. This hurt me. I was a good man – of that I was sure, although I was not in the habit of considering the morality of my actions.

'So what makes you so grand,' I attacked. 'So what makes you so fucking superior? You don't know anything about me!'

'No indeed,' he said in the same tired voice, and he seemed not to have any interest in me and perhaps momentarily in anything else, as if he had suddenly discovered the complete inadequacy of his powers.

'You think I'm not interested in history, for example.'

He looked up again and said emphatically, 'You are not.'

'But I am,' I retorted sharply. 'In fact I have two tickets to a Fukuyama. Perhaps you would like to come?'

'Nobody goes to Fukuyamas any more. The authorities don't encourage it. Once they liked to prove to people how well off they were by showing them the age of history at the Fukuyamas, but now they just want us to forget about history altogether. They're just hellholes where they get the Fukuyama populations to do the few industrial jobs that still can't be done by robotised factories. They're centres of filth and misery. Who wants to go there? Besides it's not easy to get your hands on tickets these days.'

I didn't say anything because I knew he was right.

He studied me for a little while, and again this man's presence made me feel uncomfortable. His eyes were an unfocused bluish grey, his expression sad, hurt and defensive. 'Younce put you up to this, didn't he? That's why your BB went through so quickly. He has had me under surveillance for years. What is he waiting for? Why doesn't he just arrest me? He must know how many times I fart.'

I was completely out of my depth. Neither of us seemed to be playing by the rules of Machiavellian cunning generally expected in these circumstances. Always a bad liar, I was completely disarmed by his own inability to lie. I discarded all pretence at being a spy. 'He provided the tickets too.' I was to learn that this complete naivety was a most effective weapon in the spying business, as everyone mistook my honesty for genuine sympathy with their own point of view.

Linklater could not conceal his surprise. He sat heavily in his chair and stared at me again. 'Is that it? You simply admit that Younce has hired you to spy on me. That means, I suppose, that he knows less than I thought he did.' He took the tickets from my hands and studied them for no particular reason. 'Okay. Let's go to the Fukuyama on the northern section of the M25. I want you to meet someone.'

The northern section of the M25 is an endless series of malls. I was suddenly reminded that this still is a densely populated country. The motorway was crowded with lorries and vans keeping up with the voracious consumer demand of our enlightened society. The cars were few, because most people only use the mall closest to their own gated community. Life in London, with its old decaying buildings and low population, is very different from this out-of-town life, which is the norm – a norm I now found unfamiliar. Linklater, in keeping with his eccentricity, drove a battered old car of a type that had completely disappeared from our streets.

As we approached the Fukuyama, we saw its perimeter fence, the surveillance towers and the police patrols. Linklater took the slip road and made his way to the car park in a manner that suggested familiarity with the layout. A large but dilapidated welcome sign towered over the entrance: 'Welcome to Fukuyama End-Of-History Theme Park No. 5 – Franchised by Happy History Inc. the company that makes history fun for all the family'.

'That notice must have been there for thirty years,' said

Linklater. 'These Fukuyamas used to be genuine fun parks, but now they're basically detention centres for uncarded human stock.'

'What do you mean?'

'Well, not everyone knows that the fertility of people fitted with Rational Consumer Implant Cards is incredibly low, so our society needs to regularly top up our population with people from here. They have the implant operation and then go on an induction course. In other words they become good consuming citizens of our Federation. These Fukuyamas originally came from America and are now being introduced on continental Europe as well.'

'In the European Union?' I asked.

'Yes, that's right. Of course RCI cards are still optional over there. The Europeans more or less follow everything the Federation does, but with a little less enthusiasm – which is, I suppose, a small mercy – a relative good. But then again, the fundamentals are the same. And they profit from the Federation's treatment of the Third World without getting their hands dirty.'

'The Third World?'

'We'll talk about these things another time. I want to introduce you to someone.'

We showed our tickets to a bored-looking man with a dark handsome face. He wore what Linklater later told me was a three-cornered hat. 'Hello, Linklater, are you the only person who ever comes for a fun day out? I see you've brought someone else along. Come to see how the other half live, have we? Linklater, you're going to get into trouble sooner or later. Wake up to the truth. There are plenty of informers in here, you know. You're naive to think that we are all honest just because we don't consume. Sentimental claptrap. Half the people in here would give their right arm to be carded and become citizens. There's more corruption in here than out there where you lot come from. Corruption, you see, requires a little inventiveness.'

'Not a comparison you're in a position to make, and it's a risk I'm willing to run,' Linklater cut him short and clearly showed he did not enjoy the man's company.

'Stay away, Linklater,' the man spat his words contemptuously. 'We're not interested in your politics in here. I might hate the regime as much as you do, but for very different reasons. It isn't the repression that matters – it is the way we live now: so distant from intricacy, so distant from bewilderment, so distant from unhurried reflection on a sound, a series of words or a fading colour. We do so little, and when we do something, we do it too quickly. Here at least we Fukuyama people still invent a little, make do and fill our time with thoughts within our little cage. But don't free us to be like you, Linklater! We are freer in our prison. Creativity, Linklater! You'll never understand it.'

'Creativity,' Linklater pronounced slowly and dismissively, to emphasise that he had been dragged into an argument he did not want to examine, 'is one of those meaningless words.'

'Like freedom,' the man in the three-cornered hat snapped back.

'I can't stand that little parasite', Linklater said once we were out of the man's hearing, 'if you ask me, he's the informer that is dogging our every move.'

'How can you be sure?'

'I can't.'

'Rather an obvious place to put an informer. And shouldn't informers be ingratiating?'

'Possibly,' said Linklater pensively. 'Maybe it is wrong to believe that enemies should be dislikeable and friends likeable.'

I had now been in the Fukuyama long enough to notice that all its inmates were wearing strange clothes. Some were wearing helmets, some were carrying plastic swords, some had strange hats and pistol belts and some sported once colourful military uniforms, but all these items were as worn as the expressions on people's faces. We stopped at a coffee shop consisting of a tiny room with a few rusting tables outside, and were served by a fat and wordless woman in peasant clothes of a type used in the history period.

'The idea was simplicity itself,' Linklater took on his didactic tone; 'we live in a period when history has stopped, a reality that is completely homogeneous in both temporal and spatial terms. What was needed at the beginning of the End-of-History period was a presentation of the history period as an equally homogeneous period, so all eras and epochs were mixed up together and became one. Generally speaking, they only retained their most negative elements in order to show history in the worst possible light and the End-of-History in the best.

'You asked about the Third World: well that's the part of the world where history hasn't ended. Francis Fukuyama, the philosopher after whom these places were named, talked a lot about the Universal and Homogeneous State, but he also said that for some time, the world will be divided into what he calls a "post-historical part", in which we are lucky enough to live, and a part that is "stuck in history", the part we call the Third World. It was therefore felt that asylum-seekers from countries that were stuck in history could make themselves useful by enacting history for the benefit of citizens of the post-historical world. In Fukuyamist terms, these people inhabit a limbo between the historical hell and the post-historical paradise.'

As we drank our tasteless tea, a young woman came round the corner and headed straight for us. She sat down and looked around nervously. 'Did anyone follow you?'

Linklater ignored the question. 'Edith, I want you to meet this young man. He has been engaged by Captain Younce to spy on us, and I thought he might be able to return the compliment.'

'How can we trust him?'

'I am a good judge of character,' he said with untypical confidence.

'Excuse me, if I'm not overly impressed,' said Edith. I had never been a womaniser, and apart from Constantia I had not had any long-term relationships. Besides, that only lasted a year. It seemed to me that the time had come to relax and start enjoying life. The attractive woman across the pitted and rusting wrought-iron table was a place to start. Strictly speaking, citizens are not allowed to have sexual relations with Fukuyama inmates, but my BB protected me from rules like that. Her determination to treat me with utter contempt only increased her attraction.

'I have a Berlusconi Bonus.'

'Do you now?' she persisted in her scornful tone.

'I could be useful to you.'

'That depends on who you are.'

'Come on, Edith,' said Linklater, 'give the man a chance.'

'He'll have to prove himself.'

'How?' asked Linklater.

She turned to me in a businesslike manner: 'We are attempting to co-ordinate resistance from all the various Fukuyamas. It is not at all easy, as these human dumping grounds are scattered over the country. On the other hand, Fukuyama people are more skilled and resourceful than your average carded citizen – that includes the police. So we can get messages around in the delivery vans that collect goods undergoing particular production cycles in the Fukuyamas. Do you get my drift?'

Actually, I didn't. I was struggling with all the information that I was required to digest, information of three different orders. Younce provided me with concepts of state security and spying, Linklater provided me with historical insights totally unknown to our society, and now Edith was talking the language of clandestine subversion. This last category was the most unnerving. I am not a man of great courage. Even as a businessman, I was never a real risk-taker. Although I had bent the rules on occasions, my financial success was not primarily built on sharp dealings but rather on a careful and methodical study of the market. In that sense, I might have been considered an ideal citizen of the Federation and a living example of its values and beliefs. I now consider that ideal to be a complete myth. The reality of the way the Federation is run is that spivs, risk-takers and rule-breakers are the real winners. And behind them work the dark forces of a state that is all the more terrifying for the hidden way in which it manages to carry out its tasks with great expertise and efficiency.

It was agreed that I was to pick up Edith close to the perimeter fence, from which she somehow seemed quite confident of escaping, and take her to another Fukuyama where we would meet some fellow conspirators. Linklater showed a complete disinterest in the mechanics of rebellion and did not rejoin the conversation until we had finished with the practical details. He laid out *The Sun Newspaper – Voice of the Federation in its crusade against the axis of evil*. 'Another explosion,' he announced gravely, pointing to a photograph. 'And this time we have a witness,' he pointed to me.

'Oh yeah!' said Edith suspiciously.

'This is important,' he continued, 'because for many years we have been looking for witnesses to such atrocities. What happened to the dead and wounded? What happened to the other witnesses around you?' I explained the whole incident much as I have already done in these notes. I was honest and Linklater seemed to appreciate that. Edith, on the other hand, retained her suspicions and clearly wanted to bring the conversation back under her control.

'The significant fact,' she cut in, 'is not the treatment of witnesses but the occurrence of a similar explosion on exactly the same date last year.'

Federation newspapers only carry the day and the month of publication. I remember from my childhood that newspapers did once show the year, but then the Federation announced that it made no sense having years in the End-of-History. 'If they go on like this,' argued Linklater, 'they will end up with newspapers that are identical to the same day of the previous year. But I can see no great advantage to the authorities.'

'Oh I can,' countered Edith emphatically. 'To start with, they will cut costs and eliminate a whole series of professions. There will be no more need for editors, sub-editors, journalists, photographers, etc., and more importantly the public will be led through an identical seasonal narrative every year. Think how reassuringly cyclical that will be. Nothing too bad can happen, because nothing too bad happened last year. By nothing too bad, I mean nothing that will really upset the comfortable realities of life in the Federation.'

This left me in a state of confusion. What was the relationship between these people and the explosion? Younce would want to know. I asked who they thought could have committed such an outrage. They appeared genuinely surprised and perhaps a little irritated by the question. They both thought that the government was the most likely culprit, but it could not be excluded that there was indeed some mad terrorist group going around setting off bombs. 'One thing is certain,' Linklater again in didactic mode, 'it had nothing to do with either Saddam Hussein or Osama bin Laden as the paper claims, because short of discovering the elixir of life and living longer than Methuselah, both men must have died long ago.' Linklater really was an oddball. Words like 'elixir' and 'Methuselah' simply no longer exist in our vocabularies. The man became my university, although Younce did play his part too. It was a crash-course in reality. My education at school had consisted entirely of the normal End-of-History subjects like business ethics, management mathematics, consumer logic, pricing, stock-marketology, transcendental trading and media studies. Linklater was to open up a whole universe, but at this stage I was still resistant to what I considered an affectation.

'Nor can it have been anything to do with Al-Qaeda,' Linklater continued, 'as all Muslims were either massacred or expelled from the Federation in 2011. It was one of the most shameful moments in our history, on a par with the crimes committed against European Jews and Gypsies in the history period. As with Jews in the 1930s, Muslims were supposed to be involved in an international plot that was both secret and yet inclusive of every single Muslim living in the Federation – and there were millions of them at the time. If such an organisation still exists, it is highly unlikely that it could penetrate Western society.'

CHAPTER FOUR

The Tryst

IF YOU HAVE seen one Fukuyama, you have seen them all. The same ridiculous clothes, the same sad faces, the same sense of people in limbo, waiting for a chance to be taken in as citizens. Of course, we think of ourselves as normal and the Fukuyama people as completely abnormal. But they are as nature made them, while our thought processes are filtered through a Rational Consumer Insert Card that attempts to deaden all thoughts that go beyond the logic of enlightened self-interest. The Last Man, as Fukuyama defined the ideal type we have become, turned out to need a little help from technology. I now know that the problem had always been how to create an economic model that works when people – that is, uncarded people – are so innately incapable of acting rationally or consistently in their own economic self-interest. Yes, economic self-interest has always been a powerful motivator, but never the sole one. First comes along the sexual drive and knocks it clean out of the ring. And that is just looking at the crudest level. Then comes what I would now call the pleasure of creativity: the human need to create something meaningful. Quite irrational. Rather than consuming, people really like creating something and presenting it for the admiration of others. The free-marketeers would consider this puerile and selfish, but then they have a knack of reducing every human passion to its basest interpretation. Without this creative passion, I believe we would have none of the beautiful things created in the history period. Then comes human solidarity: compassion for other people's sufferings. This really sets the economists' teeth on edge. What! You abhor the famine caused by the high price of wheat and rice. You don't want us to invade some little country, terrorise the population and install a dictatorship so that we can have cheap oil, coffee, cocoa, tea and ethnic canvas bags! It is do-gooders like you that upset the whole natural balance of the economy. I might share your concerns, I might even commend them, but the free market has been decreed by the End-of-History, and who are we mere individuals to question the mysteries of its inner workings.

Then comes religion with its often senseless rules and demands for altruistic behaviour. Strangely the neoliberals of the New Liberty Party and the neoconservatives of the New Freedom Party have always held religion very dear, but they stop at allowing its dictates to go beyond looking after one's own soul and its salvation; it appears that enlightened self-interest is as important in the next world as it is in this one. Raising questions of poverty in some forgotten corner of the world is considered an act of moral self-indulgence. I remember these things from when I was doing Transcendental Trading at school. They taught us that heaven is really a kind of celestial stock exchange in which your share values can go up and down. If you're into transcendentalism, then follow whatever religion you like and build up your share values by doing the right thing, as long as this does not interfere with the right of other citizens to consume – the most sacrosanct right of all.

And then, after religion, comes irrationalism pure and simple: the real buggeration factor, the sheer unpredictability of the human mind.

This is why the utilitarian ideologues, or rather the cleverer scientists who worked for them, came up with the RCI cards. The Rational Consumer Implant Cards iron out all the uncertainty and irrationality. The brain is wonderfully transformed into a computer that records the price for every item and systemises the central and complex task of consumption. This in turn stimulates the economy in all the right directions. It is also very useful because it kills off the creative instinct and the wasteful habit of collecting information that has no economic purpose. It was this invention that really destroyed history, which our free world had scorned for a long time. Linklater once told me that the term 'End-of-History Period' was not actually adopted as an official term until about twenty years after the first Declaration of the End-of-History. Then it was applied in a more limited way and basically meant that humanity had now discovered its ideal way of living: namely the liberal free-market democratic state (democratic as long as it voted for free-market liberalism). It appears, then, that even the 'End-of-History' has had a complex historical evolution.

Edith took me to a concrete-block house in Fukuyama End-Of-History Theme Park No. 18. It was somewhat larger than the other hovels and had two floors. Downstairs there was a single room with a staircase, and upstairs two bedrooms. Edith seemed rather proud of it, and I soon realised that she must have spent quite a lot of time there. She patted the cushions, straightened the furniture and closed the curtains carefully. She made coffee of surprisingly good quality, and sat down close to me on a rather tasteless but nevertheless quite new sofa. All the time she talked, but not of the serious questions that were supposed to concern us. Did I like folk music? Did I like jazz? She really liked jazz. Had I seen *The Forsyte Saga*, that weird television series from the history period? What were those people like? Really? At the time, I thought she was speaking like that because she knew I wasn't really interested in politics or history, although my interest in the latter was beginning to grow.

After a bit, I was struck by the oddness of the situation. She had gone to all the trouble of breaking out of a Fukuyama theme park, and breaking into another with me in tow, and now she just wanted to discuss CDs and television programmes. And where were our fellow conspirators? When I raised my doubts with her, she swivelled round on the sofa and her beautiful piercing blue eyes gave their reply. I found it difficult to return her gaze, the strength of her gaze, but my fascination with her had now reached the point where even a man with an RCI card stuffed firmly in the middle of his brain begins to feel a degree of irrationalism creep up on him and hijack his thoughts. She stared at me for a long time, and to me it seemed even longer. It was both unnerving and titillating. Now even I knew where we were going, and I started to take in the soft curve of her neck, the roundness of her breasts, the neatness of her waist, the understated but still generous form of her thighs, and all the other little triggers of male sexual desire.

'I cancelled. I told the others we would meet some other time.' She made a circular movement of her hand to suggest the vagueness of a possible future encounter. 'I want to be alone with you. In fact, I want you, Adolphus; I want to make love to you and I've wanted that since the minute I set eyes on you.'

Now men tend to believe what they want to believe, particularly when it comes to a beautiful woman making declarations of love, but a man as plain as I am could not think that a woman like Edith would fall hopelessly in love with him – not an overweight man of a distinctly pasty complexion with a wart on the left side of a large and slightly asymmetrical nose. It defied the laws of probability and could only mean one thing: Linklater had asked her to seduce me and win me over to their cause. That was fine by me. I would let them think I was putty in their hands and then report everything back to Younce. I would be fucking her out of a sense of patriotic duty. She was beautiful, she was exciting, she was dangerous – exactly as all women should be in spy thrillers.

Edith led me upstairs into a bedroom which was also furnished with cheap but new flatpack furniture of the type you would not expect to find in a Fukuyama, where everything is improvised. Unlike sex in spy thrillers, our physical union was fumbling, passionless and perfunctory. Afterwards, she spoke very little and I could feel that she wanted to leave. That hurt me, but I too was at a loss for words. She did however say one thing that was very strange. She asked me to lie to Linklater and tell him that we had met five members of a local resistance group with whom we were drawing up plans for non-violent sabotage. Linklater, it turned out, was big on non-violent protest. If Linklater was not to know about what happened, how could he be behind my seduction?

Then, as fully dressed Edith stood before me and shook her body impatiently as though to say let's get going, I realised that far from fucking for the Federation, I had fallen in love. That too was to be my undoing.

CHAPTER FIVE

Withholding from Younce

THE OFFICES OF the CSA are imposing, aggressively imposing. They hug the riverfront on a bend, and rise up in a semicircle so that they immediately close in around you and trap you against the river. The building has a heavy granite facade, an endless expanse of stone and apparently tiny windows. The overall effect is that it can see you but you cannot see into it. Inside it is all corridors and lifts, aluminium and marble – well scrubbed but no sign of anyone doing the scrubbing. This is unusual nowadays, when nearly all public buildings are dirty and you occasionally meet some desultory gang of cleaners from a Fukuyama or common prison, organised of course by a private agency, probably the same one that runs the prison or Fukuyama.

I was taken straight to Captain Younce's office and saw no one on the way. Nevertheless I felt that this was one part of the Lean State that functioned very well indeed, and Younce was clearly high up in the hierarchy, although I had few indicators to go by beyond the deference of the guard who took me to his room. The office was massive, more like a flat. At one end I could see a separate room that had been fitted out as a gym. At the other I could see a kitchen and a bedroom. The main reception room was massive, as was his desk which faced the river. It was a beautiful object made of exquisite wood and intricately carved. 'Indian', he said, as though I should know that this meant something very special. 'Hand-carved.'

He circled the desk, sat down and indicated for me to sit down in front of him with my back to the river. Again I felt trapped. I hadn't prepared my story. Or rather, I had prepared it but was unsure whether I would be able to stick to it when faced with Younce's steely gaze. 'So what do we have to report.'

'Well, I visited the Fukuyama, as you commanded.'

'Commanded?' he retorted. 'I never command a free citizen to do anything. How many people did you and Linklater meet at the Fukuyama?'

'Well, none really sir.'

'Do not sir me. You have a BB and are not in the employ of the CSA,' he commanded with false magnanimity. 'Did you or did you not meet someone at the Fukuyama?'

'Well, only a middle-aged man in a three-cornered hat.'

Captain Younce's eyes sparkled with suppressed anger. He had clearly understood that I was lying. 'A quarter of the population of the Fukuyamas wear three-cornered hats. In your opinion, was this middle-aged man a member of a subversive organisation?'

'He may have been.'

'What did you talk about?'

'The existence of informers in the Fukuyamas.'

'Really?' Younce showed a little more interest. 'And where did you meet the gentleman with the three-cornered hat?'

'At a dilapidated old bar with rusting tables.' I was trying to get away with half-truths but clearly it wasn't working, for no sooner did these words leave my mouth than Younce threw back his chair in an act of impatience. He then marched his assertive march towards a closed door. 'Follow me,' he said without looking at me, and I did his bidding as though pulled by a string. He opened the door and took me into a spacious study whose walls were lined with books. He turned on me just as abruptly as his departure, and said, 'Mr Hibbert, I am a busy man and we are not playing games here. The security of the Federation is at stake. I require you to give me detailed and above all accurate information. It is for me to decide what is relevant and what is not. Do I make myself clear?'

He then paused and seemed to calm down a bit before continuing. 'Look, I know this must all be very new to you, so I am willing to make an exception this time, but remember once you have started working for the CSA, you remain an operative until we no longer need your services. And I don't care whether you have a BB or not. You are entering a new world, a world of ideas, a battle of ideas, a battle between good and evil.' And as he said these words, he indicated his bookshelves with a sweep of the hand. 'The RCI card overrides our irrational impulses, but at times of heightened awareness or particular stress, it sometimes fails to act as effectively as it should. It may be that by throwing you in at the deep end, as it were, I have exposed you to experiences that have interfered with your normal behaviour as a citizen and rational consumer. You may have become aware of realities that to the superficial eye appear unjust. I can understand this reaction and I might even commend it, if it weren't so dangerous to the community as a whole.

'Listen to me carefully,' he continued. 'The books on this side of my study are evil. They represent the thoughts of our enemies, and as a guardian of our free society I am obliged to read and study them. Here we have Marx, a defective mind if ever there was one. Here we have the Koran, the teachings of a religion that is inherently inimical to the workings of liberal capitalism. Here is Gandhi, a romantic leader and believer in non-violent protest, the most dangerous kind of all.'

That was the second time I had heard of non-violence. This meant that Linklater was one of the most dangerous elements around. Keen to ingratiate myself, I decided to come clean on this particular piece of significant data. 'Linklater is a supporter of non-violent protest.'

The captain turned to me wearily. 'Did he tell you this himself?'

'No.'

'Then who did?'

'The man in the three-cornered hat.'

'Ah him, of course. I'd have him arrested straightaway, if only I knew which three-cornered hat.' He harrumphed to show either disbelief or impatience. 'Here we have the exponents of liberation theology, people who go around cruelly raising the hopes of people in the Third World.'

The Third World was constantly being mentioned, and my understanding was gradually growing. I was interested in what his interpretation would be, but I decided that it would best just to listen to his lecture and then hopefully he would let me go.

'On the other side of my study, we have those who wrote for the good of humanity and not to distract it from its natural instincts of self-betterment and the pursuit of wealth and happiness. We have the great utilitarian thinkers of the nineteenth century.'

I noticed that he was not afraid of referring to specific historical periods.

'They are all a little suspect,' he continued, 'but they are a good starting point. The nineteenth century also produced Hegel, who understood both the state and the spirit that inexorably moves history along its preordained route. Then we have a great man like Malthus, who understood the basic demographic problems of economics, the rules that cannot and should not be tampered with. And of course, moving quickly on, we have Fukuyama himself who, with a few suggestions from Kojève, so cleverly established that paradise on earth was not some distant nirvana as in Marxism, but the here and now of our own liberal society. Both utopias involved a withering-away of the state, only Marx's still had to do its withering whereas Fukuyama's had got ahead of the game and withered already.'

'What are utopias?' I finally had to ask.

'Yes, indeed,' he responded pleasantly. 'No-places of dreamt-up perfection. Utopias have a lot to answer for; that is, utopias set in the future,' he unconvincingly corrected himself for the sake of orthodoxy. 'It is strange that utopias were invented once the pace of change started to quicken in the middle of the last millennium, because if ever the idea of a utopia had a chance of working, it would be in a period of unchanging conditions in which the future could be planned. We have conjured up a synthetic utopia for the present day by pretending that conditions never change. Self-delusion? Yes, I suppose it is, but our self-delusion is at least more honest than that of revolutionaries and dreamers.'

At the time his whole argument went right over my head, but now that I reflect on it, I feel that Younce was not entirely wrong: how can you build a model for a future whose conditions could be so different? Problems of survival could be more acute, resources could be less abundant, epidemics could create a shortage of manpower, or a further wave of mechanisation could lead to an even greater surplus of manpower. Politicians and administrators want power, and work with the real materials of ·today, but political thinkers and utopian dreamers try to get control of the chaotic and elusive contingencies of tomorrow. Anyone who attempts to predict the future is a fool, possibly a dangerous and irresponsible one. The warring factions of one generation often have more in common with each other than with any of the warring factions of the next generations. And yet I think there is a general and aesthetic truth that holds good for all humanity throughout its generations. But don't ask me what that truth is, and distrust all those who claim to hold it up while decrying relativism in a strident voice and a warlike manner.

'Adolphus, I want you to meet someone who will help you with the plethora of strange ideas that you are suddenly confronted with. His name is Michael Foxtrotter. He is what is called an official dissident. There is a market for dissident thoughts, and we would be failing in our duties as a consumer society if we did not provide for that demand. We therefore have official dissidents who write for papers like *The Guardian*, and criticise the government and indeed the opposition as well, but always within the limits of sensible, responsible and honest debate. For instance, Foxtrotter will say that not enough is being done to level up the economic playing field between the rich countries of the West and the poor countries of the Third World, but he would never dream of giving them aid. If the Federation has to invade some Third-World country to defend our strategic interests, then Foxtrotter can always be relied upon to give us his support with the most subtle of arguments. He is an intellectual athlete. I have read all his books, and although I do not really hold with all of it, there is nothing that I find too disturbing. I feel that he might be of help in your case, because someone like you could easily have his head turned by a fanatic like Linklater.

'A final word of warning. Do not enter into sexual relations with any of the malcontents that you come across in your work for the CSA. I refer to the female ones of course, as your file has you down as heterosexual. If, however, you do succumb to some woman's charms, then you must avoid becoming emotionally involved. Think of the Federation, and do whatever you have to do, but don't get emotionally involved.

'I'll set up a meeting with Foxtrotter.' The lowering tone of that final sentence announced that the interview was over. The guard appeared and I was soon out on the street. My confusion was further increased.

CHAPTER SIX

The Berlusconi Bonus Club

I DID NOT see Edith between our lovemaking and my summons to the CSA headquarters. Little happened during that period, although I did report to Linklater in true spy fashion. We met in a park, sat on a bench and I told him that we had met five conspirators willing to do anything to bring down our repressive regime. Linklater was not happy. He did not want anything violent. He wanted a well-thought-out campaign that did not endanger anybody's life but hit the economy and forced the government to listen to our demands, which were, he said, the integration of all the Fukuyama populations into the rest of society, the destruction of the Theme Parks which were no more than detention camps, an undertaking never to go to war except in self-defence, and the right of all citizens to remove their RCI cards. That would do for starters, he chortled. But then he too started acting funny and asked me to describe the five men. He might have known them, he claimed. He kept on picking over things. What did I think of Edith? Ah, I thought, he *is* the one who put her my way; he *is* trying to manipulate me. And that was it. Linklater told me to lie low for a bit and get on with enjoying my BB or whatever I liked doing. He would contact me in due course.

That is exactly what I did. Perhaps I should describe my experiences during this relative lull in my story in the run-up to the unnerving encounter with Younce that I have already described.

The BB Club is a plain building on the outside, and the nameplate declares that it is The Society for the Betterment of Third-World Students, complete with charity registration number. But once your membership card has made the front door open, you enter a world of comfort, opulence and waste that is quite giddying. We claim to be a society of choice, but one mall is pretty much like another. Company names change and strident advertising makes great claims, but most products are exactly the same as their equivalents from the corporate competition. The first day I went through the door of No. 55 The Strand into the Berlusconi Bonus Club, I discovered the real meaning of choice, discrete choice that awaits the unhurried and natural maturation of your desires. It takes a little time to understand how to use the endless delights contained beyond that door which leads not just into the building behind but all the buildings in the street, each with its false purpose inscribed on a brass plate. Wealth is freedom, liquid freedom. The first night I entered was like discovering the vastness of the world and the variety of its pleasures. They were all at my disposal and my youth would provide me with more than enough time to discover them one by one. They were not pushed on me as are the dubious tacky pleasures of our consumer society; they were simply there like ripe fruit in a bowl, to be taken or to be left in the certain knowledge that they would be replaced with equally ripe fruit the following day. The BB Club was the paradise that our consumer society claims to be, and isn't. It was an Eden of plenitude.

The Club contained restaurants, bars, gyms, massage parlours, swimming pools, libraries, brothels, dancehalls, marriage bureaus, dating agencies, psychiatric services, legal firms, debating halls, cinemas, theatres, chapels and funeral services. It organised excursions, study trips, language classes, lectures, banquets, encounters with politicians, and religious retreats. Above all, it provided exclusivity and delightful security and intimacy for the very rich.

One evening when I entered, a man called Priapus Smith was just before me in the lobby. I had met him on a few occasions, and he was a small wiry middle-aged man whose persistent friendliness and apparent desire to please hid a mischievous sense of humour. He asked me a lot of questions about myself with a look of fascinated rapture but always greeted my answers with a kind of forgetful disappointment. The incongruence between the active and passive parts of his conversation probably never occurred to him. Wealth does not bring self-knowledge; indeed it probably impedes it. 'My lad, my lad,' he cried enthusiastically, 'how long have you been a BB?' When I told him it was nearly three months, he treated the information as either irrelevant or unreliable, and jumped to the next question. 'Have you been enjoying the good weather?' I told him I had. 'Good, good,' he said absentmindedly, 'now exactly what was it that you made your money from?'

I told him.

'Augustus,' he said, 'I've been meaning to ask you – if you don't mind – but are you what they call a married man?'

'It's Adolphus,' I responded, not without a hint of irritation in my voice, 'and no, I'm not married.'

'Ah!' he said holding his mouth open and looking up at me with what bizarrely resembled surprise or perhaps doubt. He appeared to be heaving a really difficult piece of information into his brain. 'Adolphus, you say,' he finally uttered, clearly having decided to take my word for it, and then more brightly, 'but not married! Well, that's okay then, isn't it? I mean – I've been meaning to tell you that there is an awfully good brothel in this place. A young man like you should be using it. Damn it, if an old fart like me is down there practically every night of the week, then what is a young blade like yourself doing? You're not one of those pansies, are you? Are you?'

'No,' I replied in a tired voice.

'Then what are we waiting for? Christ, man! What were we put in this world for, if it wasn't to have a little fun?' And he grabbed me by the arm and pulled me along what was clearly for him a very familiar route. The brothel area itself was a series of corridors where the prostitutes sat and exhibited themselves behind glass panes. On one side, there were women dressed in various garments designed to titillate men, although many were too absurd to achieve their aim. On the other side, the women wore extravagant clothes from the history period, and there were little plaques beneath to explain their historical period and provenance: 'Aristocrat of the English Regency period', 'Persian Harem, eighteenth century', 'German peasant woman, fourteenth century', and so on. They sat like so many dolls in an antique shop. Sexual toys presented as old curiosities. I chose the 'Senator's wife from Republican Rome'. She wore a white dress which gathered its cloth together above the shoulder, leaving the arms and most of the shoulder bare. It then came back together immediately under the breasts which were made the central attraction, and then flowed outwards down past the knees. Her skin was almost as white as her dress, and the only contrasting items were her red lips, her black sandals and her even blacker and beautifully made-up hair. There was something in her understatedness I found very attractive, so I pressed the red selection button set in the mahogany frame just below the exhibition pane. She immediately stood up to come and greet me, while flashing a cool professional smile in my direction. She took me through to a large sumptuous bedroom in the late-eighteenth-century, neo-classical style (which was used throughout of the BB Club). The four-poster bed looked invitingly comfortable with its scarlet linen and carefully arranged cushions, but she guided me to a chaise-longue, sat me down and, while she ruffled my hair in an almost maternal manner, she asked me if I would like a drink.

When she returned with a gin and tonic, she had the look of a person whose professional standards have been offended: 'I'm very sorry but the computer isn't showing anything for your musical tastes.'

'That's probably because I don't really have any. Never had time...' I started apologetically, but she cut me short.

'No, don't worry about that. I'll choose for you. Many of my customers find jazz from the late period very soothing, so we'll start there and just tell me if you want to change it – or anything else. I'm here to make your evening a happy one.' Music was provided, and I began to enjoy the sweet unhurriedness of it all. The whole thing was clearly the product of long experience and considerable attention to detail on the part of management and staff.

She sat down next to me on the chaise-longue. Both her closeness and her distance seemed equally erotic: I could feel the heat from her body, I could smell her delicate perfume that did not entirely mask a young woman's warm scent, and I could just hear her regular and highly controlled breath. She put her hand in mine and said, 'Adolphus, tell me about yourself – that is if you want to. And any time you want to go to bed, just say so. Tell me, Adolphus, what is it you do?' Even though this was clearly how she dealt with all her customers, her rich BB customers, there was something reassuringly pleasant about the entire procedure. I told her. Yes, I told her. I sat there and talked about my trading in hospital supplies to a beautiful woman dressed up beautifully in some ancient garb in a luxurious room with a four-poster bed. Occasionally she would squeeze my hand or smile at me and say, 'Adolphus, that is really incredible. I have never spoken to anyone about the price of bedpans before. I never knew they could be such fascinating things. And the idea of a disposable inner lining is superb.'

At the time, it never occurred to me to think about what her comments would be when, at the end of her evening's work, she returned to wherever and whoever she returned to. She was completely convincing. No, not completely. You cannot have that degree of carefully, wonderfully honed professional self-control and be completely convincing, but you are the best surrogate for it. And you can't buy the real thing, so this was the best money could buy.

I might have talked about Free Market Super-Saver Trust Hospitals all evening and all night, but at precisely the moment when I realised I did not know how to steer the conversation in other directions, she skilfully slipped her hand under my shirt and said with controlled breathlessness, 'You're not going to keep a poor girl waiting, are you?' She seemed to strip the clothes off me quite effortlessly and as she went she complimented my body, which frankly is rather flabby and unhealthily white. She then moved me to the bed and moved my hands under her skirt and against her body.

It was at that moment that a memory came back to me, a memory that had been completely ignored for a long time, possibly since its inception. There is an area around Dartford that is very poor, well poor by our standards. Most of the people who live there are in receipt of citizens' relief, which ensures they have enough means to engage with our consumer democracy. These people have no rich parents to buy them into decent colleges, no capital for making more capital. Their one important task is to provide a market for a mass of cheaply produced goods, but crime rates are high and drug addiction rife. Drugs are seen as a terrible threat by the authorities: their presence is unsurprising in a society that worships consumption, but they distort the market, override RCI cards and force the Federation into half a dozen drug wars in the Third World in any given moment. When I was seventeen I took the considerable risk of visiting this area to see Katy, a girl with a drug problem who was well known to my schoolmates for selling the pleasure of fucking her.

When I got to her flat in a decaying concrete block, the door was already open. I entered and there was a man, possibly Katy's father, who was lying on a sofa, watching the television and drinking beer with a little difficulty as each swig required the great effort of raising his head by about two inches. 'What the fuck do you want?' he said in an aggressive voice that may well have been his only register.

'I wanted to see Katy,' I answered nervously.

'The fucking whore's through there. Now piss off!'

I quickly moved through the door he had pointed to, but found myself in a corridor with several more doors.

'Down the back, right to the end, you prick,' I could hear him shouting from the sitting room. I then heard him mutter to himself, 'Little pricks in and out of that door all day long - you'd think the bastards owned the place. Not an ounce of sense in one of them.'

I moved to the end of the corridor and knocked softly on the door, both frightened and expectant.

'Who the fuck is there?' came the uninviting response.

'Adolphus, a friend of Maximus.'

'Who the fuck is Maximus?'

'You know Maximus; goes to the Donald Rumsfeld Spirit of Free Enterprise School in Upminster.'

'Never heard of the bastard. But who cares anyway. Come

in, you little wanker and get on with it.'

I entered the room and there she was sitting on the edge of the bed in a dressing-gown looking really tired. It was as though the tiredness had drained everything out of her: her intelligence, her curiosity, her feeling, her hope, her love, her life. She was thin. Very thin. She had nice features but they were marred by a quantity of spots and a really painful-looking black eye. 'You know the score?' she asked. I nodded my consent. 'That means no funny business, and no hanging about afterwards.' Again I confirmed my agreement without uttering a word. The room was filthy, and the only decoration some posters of pop stars that were almost in shreds. Garments littered the floors, along with a few syringes and a few cosmetics covered with grease, dust and hairs. 'That'll be five dollars up front.' I handed over the money, and she immediately removed her dressing-gown and lay back on the grimy bed. 'Get a move on then!' Which is what I did with very little assistance from her. When it was over and she said, 'Well, that was a lot of fuss about nothing,' I felt a certain compassion for her, and perhaps a little guilt. 'Can I come back to see you another time?' I heard myself mutter.

'Just so long as you bring your money.'

'But I would – I would really like to know you...'

She then leapt from the bed and shouted, 'I thought I told you no hanging about, no fucking hanging about here – right! Get out of my fucking room, you creep.' Without bothering to close her dressing-gown, she pushed me out of the door. I left my dignity behind in her room along with my virginity.

That was the memory that came back to me with a wave of belated shame just as the Roman senator's wife attempted to suck my erect penis. I pushed her away gently. Why should she do this? Why was she doing this?

'Do you want to enter straightaway?' she asked without expressing any surprise. 'Just tell me what you would like. Don't be afraid. There are no limits here.'

'I don't want anything,' I said firmly, as I walked across the room.

'Adolphus, I can assure you that I have heard everything. Don't hold back. Let go and enjoy yourself. You're a BB; you have the right.'

She spoke calmly and the insistence in her voice was held within the limits of her exquisitely mannered approach. She walked towards me, and I said, 'It is simply that I do not want to go through with it. I don't think it is right.'

She allowed herself half a smile. 'You think it is wrong to buy love, but I am not selling you love; I am selling you a service. My only concern is to keep my customers happy. You are an important man. You have to be, otherwise you wouldn't have a Berlusconi Bonus. You are a rich and powerful man, and therefore you are also a busy man. You deserve to have sexual pleasure; it is your right, and it is my job to provide it.'

'It makes no difference,' I insisted, 'no offence to you. You are very beautiful, more beautiful than any woman I have slept with. I just don't think it's right. It's not what I want to do.'

She allowed herself another of her half smiles, her only spontaneous expressions in the whole evening. 'I said that I had heard everything, but I had never heard this. But I don't take offence. Whatever the reason for your behaviour, you are the customer and the customer is always right.'

With those words, the situation switched from something embarrassing to something deeply unpleasant. I understood even then the difference between this encounter with a prostitute and the previous one. With Katy I had entered into a transaction in which she had never ceased to be herself. She had taken control of the entire operation and never attempted to hide her utter contempt for me and all the other boys who visited her. But this woman, with her controlled and perfect manners, was completely unknown to me, and remained unknown by turning herself into an object, an object for pleasure. It is impossible to say how much was conscious in her behaviour and how much was an acquired instinct of sexual servility. Wealth might be liquid freedom, but it has a cost. It isolates you from other human beings. That evening in the company of the 'Senator's wife from Republican Rome', I learned that wealth deprives you of sincere human relationships. Even when those relationships are bad, near to worthless, a degree of sincerity means that both people can retain a degree of humanity.

Why couldn't I make love to her, while I had been able to make love to Katy in the damp and smelly backroom in Dartford? Was it that I now had a superior morality to that of my teenage self, and could no longer use a woman's body as a piece of merchandise? It would be nice to think that: we are always in search of better or even better explanations of both our bad and our good actions. It is more probable that love, the powerful, focused and so often ephemeral instinct which takes us to different kinds of thought process, was getting in the way. The clever scientists who designed the RCI cards and worked so hard to eliminate love along with all other irrational feelings, did not entirely succeed in their purpose. My love for Edith was impeding my full enjoyment of the Berlusconi Bonus and its wonderful club. My love for Edith was turning me from reliable citizen into unreliable agent of the CSA.

I took my wallet from my trousers which during her swift undressing of me she had skilfully folded onto the chaise-longue. 'Let me pay the full price,' – I attempted to adopt an air of magnanimity.

'That's alright, sir,' she replied, 'your visit has already been charged to your BB account and the bill will be sent to your accountants at the end of the month.'

CHAPTER SEVEN

The Dialogue of the Wealthy

A FEW DAYS later, after I had finished lunch at the BB Club, I saw Priapus bounding down the corridor like a man who has achieved all his ambitions in an afternoon. 'Augustus, Augustus,' he shouted, 'three in a bed – bloody fantastic; three in a bed, my lad; you should try it sometime.' He beamed at me. 'Augustus, my lad, I've been meaning to ask you: you are not, by any chance, anything to do with bedpans?' He looked at me mockingly.

'I deal in all products required by Free Market Super-Saver Trust Hospitals,' I said rather grandly.

He gave me one of his vacant pauses and then broke into an enormous smile, 'So you don't *just* do bedpans. What a pity, bedpans are so interesting. Still, I'll know where to come if I ever need one.'

He was just about to slap me on the arm and rush off when I grabbed his arm: 'Who have you been talking to?'

His shook his arm free, and for a moment his smile disappeared. 'You should cool down my friend, and learn to take a joke.' Then he transformed back to his usual ebullient self and said, 'I can get anyone to talk, me. Even a stuck-up bitch. Senator's wife, yeah? Great tits, and even better when she comes with a slave girl from Imperial Rome. I thought I should do my bit for ending class discrimination, you know. Ah! You didn't think that Priapus had it in him. You didn't think that Priapus was such a democrat, did you? A senator's wife and a slave girl having to work together.' He accompanied this with an elbow to my ribs. 'Great tits! Augustus, I've been meaning to ask you,' – I awaited some other revelation – 'are you at all interested in politics?'

'Not really,' I hesitated, a little afraid of where this was leading.

'Not really? Well that's a pity. Perhaps you should be, now that you have a Berlusconi Bonus. No, that's bullshit; politics is crap, complete crap. No, it's just that there isn't a lot to do around here – well, you know what I mean. Well not a lot to do when you're not inspecting costumes of history' – and this time a fist prodded my ribs. 'There's a debate on in the Turkish baths. Every now and then they have a debate on various political issues. I like to go along and wind those guys up, and I would really like to have the company of someone who is not really interested in politics. It'll pass the afternoon. And then we can have dinner together, and go and pick a costume. You should take the slave girl; the slave girl's a goer.'

Nobody talks politics in our society, unless you count discussing the First Lady's dress or the fact that the leader of either the New Freedom Party or the New Liberty Party is being impeached for adultery. It is not that politics is illegal in our society, as history is; it is rather that nobody knows where to start. So we find the subject slightly taboo, not good manners.

'I'll come,' I said.

'Good lad, good lad,' he put his arm in mine and led me at a brisk pace. 'Augustus, I like you. I've always said there goes a very interesting young man. Tell me, where is it you said you come from?'

'Upminster.'

'Up-min-ster', he said slowly and almost as though it were a question. 'Upminster. That's in Essex, isn't it?'

'Yes.'

'Upminster. How remarkable. You see I had an uncle who lived in Essex. He was great fun. Great fun. Bit of a ladies' man, you know. They always used to say that I took after him.'

His chatter, his pauses, his open mouth and his incredulity took us all the way to the Turkish baths. We stripped off, put on our towels and went into the part of the baths set aside for debates. It was purpose-built with seating on long rows of marble facing each other. At one end there was a single seat with lectern for the chairman, a tall, stooped and sallow man weighed down by his own gravitas. His chest was a little sunken and covered with tightly-curled, grey hair, and he had made his money by selling food products that had passed their sell-by date to the Third World. He looked on this trade as an act of charity, because he claimed that without it the feckless populations of those countries would have even higher death rates than they have already.

'Trust Priapus to turn up at the last moment,' he grumbled to the seated debaters, and then to Priapus sharply, 'No fooling around today. This is to be a serious debate. Who is your friend?'

'Augustus.'

'Adolphus, actually,' I corrected, 'Adolphus Hibbert.'

'Adolphus Hibbert,' cried the chairman. 'Good man, I knew your father. Harrow man, I was a Harrow man. You can always tell a Harrow man.'

'I don't think you could have known my father,' I protested.

'Couldn't have known his father!' Priapus exclaimed knowingly. 'Different Hibbert. You see Augustus – you say Adolphus, I could have sworn you said Augustus – Adolphus is a bit of a nouveau riche,' he grinned his malicious grin. 'Comes from Up-min-ster.' His eyes swung round the room to gauge the audience. 'Comes from Upminster and that's in Essex. A man of the people our Adolphus; a man of the people and he made his money selling bedpans to hospitals.' Again he leered his enjoyment at the debaters while searching for any curious reactions.

'I deal in all products required by Free Market Super-Saver Trust Hospitals,' I repeated my grand claim, this time in a slightly hurt tone.

'Nothing wrong with bedpans,' Priapus was now leaping gleefully between the sombre debaters who had yet to start their debate. 'Nothing wrong with bedpans. I would be damn glad of a bed-pan if I was in hospital. You wouldn't want to piss in the bed, would you? I would say that bedpans are the backbone of our Free whatever-you-call-its. Augustus, what did you say they were?'

'Free Market Super-Saver Trust Hospitals,' I said stupidly.

'Yes, Free Market... yes, yes, what you just said. Fantastic, that's what they're the backbone of. You can say no less.'

'Priapus,' said the chairman wearily, 'did you bring along your young friend simply to ridicule him? And can we now get on with the debate?'

'I would never ridicule him,' said Priapus with mock offence as he put his arm around my shoulder, 'I love the man. A shining example to our youth.'

'Before we start the proceedings,' the chairman continued, 'I would like to introduce all the debaters to our newly arrived member, Adolphus Hibbert. I am Superbus Carrington and I earned my Berlusconi Bonus producing low-cost food for poorer countries. My prime motivation was human charity and it was only by dint of hard work, imaginative manipulation of margins and inspired marketing that I managed to make any money at all. It is perhaps because of this highly developed social awareness

– typical I might say of a Harrow man – that I decided to set up this debating society specifically on political matters. Here we have Nichilaeus.' A very small, very old and very bespectacled man, whose enlarged eyes communicated complete coldness, nodded towards me very slowly. His body was almost a miniature version of Superbus'. 'He is one of the oldest BBs in the building and a very fine mind. He made his money selling arms.' Superbus collected himself with a grin to announce the delivery of a witticism, 'It has been said that he sold expensive arms at low prices to our own armed forces, and cheap arms at high prices to armed forces in the Third World, thus getting them to make a just contribution to the policing role that has been forced upon us.' Nichilaeus allowed the sides of his mouth to twitch and signal his smug appreciation of the compliment. 'His distinguished career has included advisory roles to ministers of both parties, and the Federation has awarded his Herculean efforts on many occasions. Next we have Cornelia,' and he pointed to a heavy woman with drooping jowls and sad eyes. Her towel was tied tight around her body and covered all of her large breasts. She sat upright and looked keen to get on with the business, but acknowledged the introduction by a friendly wave in my direction. 'She made her money in the retail business and worked her way up through management. Since retiring from the boards of Happy Shoppers and Low Price, she has been renowned for her equally hard work for charity and by her own admission, she only comes to these debates to put the other side of the argument and a stop to the "horrendous defamation" of the Great Fukuyama that goes on in the Turkish baths.' The other debaters grinned knowingly, with the exception of Nichilaeus who twitched his mouth. 'Next we have Penthesilea, a startling woman of strong opinions, most of which no normal intelligent human being would ever entertain.' This too was followed by knowing smiles. 'She made her money in the Official-

Dissident sector, particularly in the distribution of films from the history period that passed censor in spite of containing some rather dubious ideas. She is perhaps most famous as Michael Foxtrotter's publisher. Of course this did not make her any money as nobody reads Michael Foxtrotter.'

Here everyone laughed aloud, except Nichilaeus who simply shouted, 'Nobody reads!'

'However her contribution to the arts has been acknowledged by many governments and in spite of her many eccentricities, I for one am very much the richer for having had the pleasure, indeed the honour, of knowing her.' A galant Superbus nodded in her direction, and an entirely naked Penthesilea leapt to her feet, threw her arms straight up above her and wiggled her body in a dance of joy. She too had a thin, sinewy body which did not really deserve the extravert exhibition. 'Last but not least, we have Diogenes Jones. He didn't make his money, he inherited it.'

'And he hasn't done anything for charity,' said Diogenes himself, 'nor has he advised any government minister.'

'But he has read a lot of books, and has written quite a few as well,' Superbus took back control of the introductions. 'His reputation speaks for itself.' Diogenes was a pleasant, slightly overweight man of no more than forty years with a black beard trimmed very short. He smiled a lot and had the self-confidence of those who have never known insecurity. 'I don't expect anyone to discuss our deliberations outside the confines of the BB Club,' Superbus continued, 'because ours is a society that bases itself on self-censorship – in other words it has a responsible attitude to ideas that could be dangerous in the wrong hands. But here in this Turkish bath, everything goes.

'Right, I would like to introduce this week's session with the Great Fukuyama's quite remarkable comment on warfare, which has often been used in the context of military intervention in the

Third World. We all know the passage, but I will summarise it for you,' he looked up from his lectern to deliver the full gravity of his opinion. 'It is, after all, a concept central to the maintenance of our civilisation. According to Fukuyama, war and military competition are a great unifier of nations. It may appear that war leads to destruction, but in reality it forces states to accept modern technological civilisation and the social structures that support it. Man is unable to ignore modern natural science and the rejection of modern technological rationalism is not an option for nations that want to maintain their independence. These are profound ideas indeed. And I would not take issue with them, but I know I can count on some people here to come up with some counter-arguments. And my dear friend Nichilaeus is certainly one of them, so I would like you to start the debate off.'

Nichilaeus twitched the ends of his mouth in recognition of the 'dear friend', drew a slight breath into his slight lungs and started his lecture. 'First I will tell you what I like about Fukuyama's words. I like the fact that there is no sentimentality, none of the namby-pamby stuff you find among liberals, lefties (remember them?) and a certain kind of Christian. There is no compassion for the victims of history. Why should there be? No one, but no one can stand in the way of history. Please note that I say history and not progress.'

'Fascist!' said Penthesilea, and Superbus raised his finger for silence.

'Progress,' said Nichilaeus, 'is simply a conceit of modern man who thinks that because he has a clean shirt and clean body, he is somehow superior to his filthy, lice-infested ancestors, whereas they were probably marginally more intelligent - which is not saying that much.'

'Very nice, I'm sure,' said Cornelia; 'do you always have to be this horrid, Nichilaeus?'

'Cornelia, I am not here to be nice, but to discuss political ideas,' said Nichilaeus with the irritation of the supremely bored. 'What we have before us is not progress but a process. Every species has a lifetime, and filthy, greedy *homo sapiens* is destined to die out early, precisely because of what Fukuyama describes. His analysis is perfect, but his conclusions are not. He makes two assumptions in this passage: one that being "a great unifier of nations" is a good thing, and the other that natural science will bring benefits to mankind. Of course, I do not believe in good or bad things – I make no value judgements, because man's extinction is something of absolutely no interest to me at all, indeed its imminence is perhaps the only thing that I would consider good. The unification of nations will only put more power in fewer hands, and stupid modern man is incapable of using that power sensibly. Natural science merely increases that power even further, much further. Ladies, gentlemen and my fellow BBs,' he entered a formal conclusion, 'I say to you that it is not our business to halt the destruction of this planet, which has probably gone beyond the point of no return, but to assist it and most importantly to understand it as members of an intellectual elite. We must give assistance to power and keep the consuming masses in their current state of ignorance, out of humanity for those poor useless beings, and to protect our wonderful privilege for what remains of history.'

'A very bold and, I might say, quite unconventional view of things,' said Superbus. 'Well done, Nichilaeus; we much appreciate your intellectual depth. I would now like Diogenes Jones to give his opinion.'

Diogenes beamed pleasantly but took his time to speak. 'I am reminded,' he said with wonderful rhetorical pace, 'of the fall of the Italian republics in the early fifteenth century. You will recall, I am sure, that these republics were by far the most advanced societies in Europe at the time, but they were overwhelmed by larger countries, France and Spain, which had cruder political systems and were much further behind in the development of modern sciences. Indeed modern science was on the point of being invented at the very time that the foreign armies discovered Italy's military weakness. It is clearly not the case that militarily stronger societies are necessarily more technologically advanced. This is just one of Fukuyama's follies. In reality, he is proposing the law of the jungle: now no one would suggest that in a society of persons the biggest, strongest and best armed people should be allowed to beat up the smallest, weakest and unarmed people, and only a complete fool would suggest that this would lead to a better and more evolved society. Why then should we believe that in the society of nations the biggest, strongest and best-armed should do as they please, or that this will produce benign outcomes for humanity. If we follow the logic of Fukuyama's argument, there was nothing inherently wrong with Nazism other than the fact that it lost the war. If it had won and retained all those weak, technologically backward countries it invaded, then it would have contributed to progress and civilisation!

'So might is right for Fukuyama, but what is even more bizarre is that he believes it to be rational. Rome did not invade Gaul because of any rational plan developed by a sophisticated polity; it was tricked into the invasion by Caesar in order to further his political career and clear his debts. And the ensuing war succeeded very nicely in doing both. Eventually it also led to Caesar's early death and plunged Rome into a terrible series of civil wars that devastated Rome itself. Bush also invaded Iraq for the purposes of his political career, but he did not share the first *Imperator*'s intelligence, tactical cunning and courage to lead an army into battle. He had great difficulty in understanding that it is much easier to conquer a nation than to hold it, but we have now learned that lesson. When we attack a Third-World country, we go in hard, destroy the infrastructure and immediately withdraw. It then takes decades for that country to emerge from chaos. This is undoubtedly an effective system of control, but is it *rational*? Does it further *modern technological civilisation*? Will it provide security *indefinitely*?

'But I really want to counter Nichilaeus' idea that history is a process, and therefore by implication an inevitable process. Of course forces could change the direction of history at any time, and we would be very foolish to attempt to predict the future. We may quite reasonably express concerns about the future – for instance our treatment of the planet – but we would be wrong to imagine that anything is inevitable.'

'Excuse me Diogenes,' inquired Superbus in a concerned voice, 'but you would never entertain actively assisting in a change of direction.'

'No, I can reassure you on that point, Superbus, but honesty obliges me to confess that only cowardice and comfort restrain me. If others were to take action to improve society, I would raise no objection. The fact that I am not at all hopeful is possibly only a reflection of my own deeply pessimistic nature. But neither can I associate myself with Nichilaeus' gleeful acceptance of our problems.'

'I am glad to hear that,' pronounced the chairman, 'but before you go any further, I would like to bring in Cornelia who, like me, is a staunch defender of the Great Fukuyama.'

'It distresses me greatly to hear the Great Fukuyama's name abused once again in these Turkish Baths,' she said in an even voice that almost sounded distressed. 'We enjoy the liberties and freedoms we have today because men like Fukuyama fought for them. We personally enjoy great privilege, but with privilege comes great responsibility.'

'Fascist!' shouted Penthesilea, and Priapus dutifully backed her up with 'Bollocks!'

'I would not expect you two to understand that. I agree that there are many problems that we have to face, just as humanity has faced many problems in the past, but I also believe that with good will and hard work we can put them right. Fukuyama said, the logic of a progressive modern natural science induces...'

'How can natural science be progressive or regressive?' said Nichilaeus with exasperation. Diogenes nodded his support.

'How can anyone write, "The logical progressive modernist naturalist shit" and keep a straight face. Did Fukuyama die laughing at his own jokes?' said Priapus.

'Would you please let me speak?' she pleaded. 'Would you please let me finish what I am saying? Progressive modern natural science induces societal acceptance of capitalism only in as far as men can perceive their own economic self-interest. As only a truly liberal economy can produce a wealthy society, democracy can only really work if the population is sensible enough to support liberal economics and does not follow what Fukuyama so cleverly called "intellectual mirages". Therefore any people that does not vote for economic liberalism is automatically undemocratic and has to be abolished. We have overcome this problem in the Federation by introducing Rational Consumer Implant Cards, which predispose people to rational self-interest, and by restricting politics to a choice of two identical parties. This releases us wealthy citizens – or plutocrats as we are sometimes called – to assist the less fortunate in the certain knowledge that they will never be able to threaten our hard-won achievements.'

'Thank you for a very lucid and cogent argument. Would Penthesilea now like to say a word or two,' said the chairman, 'although I would ask her to be civil and to the point.'

'You're a bunch of fascists,' Penthesilea jumped out of her chair, 'you're a bunch of fascists. I'm the only real Fukuyamist here! I'm a revolutionary Fukuyamist!' Nichilaeus managed to mouth the last sentence to prove how often she said it. 'People either criticise Fukayama or, like Cornelia, they put their heads in the sand and say that there are no problems, but does anyone ask the important question: have we really put Fukuyama's ideas into practice? Have we truly implemented the End-of-History? I say not! We will only achieve the End-of-History when we all go out to consume and really enjoy it. Are we consuming enough? Have any of you asked that question? Diogenes just reads a lot of useless books. Not much consuming going on there. Nichilaeus is too busy planning the end of the world to do anything for the end of history. As for Cornelia, the supposed stalwart of Fukuyamism, she is too busy distorting the market by giving her money away to really help us in our revolutionary task. Consume and be happy! That is my motto. Economic self-interest is ultimately self-love, and we should not hold ourselves back.'

'No chance of that in your case,' said Nichilaeus.

'And we don't do enough for the arts,' she continued. 'We should put an end to this pretence of democracy and introduce a government of artists and economists. This would lead to a cultural revolution in which the consumer would take complete and radical control of the means of consumption.'

Everyone looked profoundly lost. 'What is this supposed to achieve,' asked Superbus drily.

'The End-of-History, you dickhead,' she shouted. 'The thing we all want.'

'But history has already ended,' pronounced Cornelia in a pained voice.

'Of course history hasn't ended,' said Diogenes briskly. 'Nor will it end. Do you think a half-baked philosopher like Fukuyama, who didn't know Hegel's arse from Kojève's elbow, could stop the seas of history like some global Moses who leads all humanity to the promised land of malls, gated communities and mountains of refuse? If he had known his Hegel, he would have known that the old man, while playing at building universes in his own authoritarian image, made the entirely correct assertion that history is a slaughterhouse. And it has continued to be one, for many have died in the name of Fukuyama's End-of-History, albeit in the Third World – so they hardly count. They do our dying for us too.'

Cornelia was beside herself with anger, and signalling frantically to the chairman while ensuring that her towel did not come undone in her agitation. At a nod from Superbus she turned icily on Diogenes, 'So are we to assume that the great Diogenes Jones is actually greater than the Great Fukuyama? So the whole of the most developed society in the history of mankind is supposed to be wrong, and Diogenes Jones who has done very little for himself and nothing for society is supposed to be right. Well,' she looked around triumphantly, as though she had actually presented an intellectual argument rather than a very pedestrian rhetorical flourish, 'what do you have to say to that, Mr Jones? Are you saying that Fukuyama was a fool and that you are a genius?'

Diogenes looked very pleased with the direction the debate was drifting in and not at all offended by the implication that he was an arrogant man. 'There is no such thing as a genius, as I have told you many times before. And Fukuyama was not a complete fool, because if you are a half-baked philosopher it is much better to write for the rich and powerful, than in search of a truth that is elusive to much cleverer men and women. That way he was able to lead a pleasant and comfortable life with recognition from his peers and above all from the powerful. I doubt that he ever dreamt that there would be such a cult attached to his name. All imperial courts have demanded the presence of sycophantic poets and scribblers. There is nothing surprising about Fukuyama's existence; what is surprising is that there weren't more people turning out his turgid and disjointed prose to better the cause of extreme capitalism.'

Cornelia was speechless with fury. Superbus invited Nichilaeus to speak. 'Very good,' came the little man's icy voice, 'very clever, silly stuff, Diogenes, but you are as usual quite wrong. In fact you are speaking complete rubbish. Man, this disgusting little creature called Man, is destroying himself, polluting the planet, and as you say, treating it as a slaughterhouse. How many generations will we last? Two, three, maybe even four. Nothing when compared to history. So you see Fukuyama was right – at least in one sense.'

Here something chilling occurred: Nichelaeus laughed or attempted to laugh. It was a hard hollow sound, a little like a cough. 'We are the Last Man because we face extinction, and not in Fukuyama's wonderfully arrogant and insouciant sense of man *in less reflective ages* testing out all possible systems of governments and finding them wanting when compared with liberal democracy. In other words, Last Man because all other types of man had been tried out and there was nowhere else to go. Last Man who has become all desire and archetypal, with a few surviving high-performers like ourselves who satisfy our desire for recognition by accumulating wealth and driving the economy. No, we are the Last Man, because Fukuyama's so-called *Liberal Democracy* is burning up the world and ridding it of the selfish little worm that is infesting it.'

'And he believed that we had achieved "absolute self-consciousness",' spluttered Diogenes.

'And he believed that our society is democratic and liberal,' laughed Penthesilea, 'but that was a minor oversight compared with the brilliance of abolishing history. The sheer audacity of it.' Even Nichilaeus touched his stomach as though his imaginary laughter was getting too much for him.

Cornelia looked like a woman whose God's name had been taken in vain. 'I don't know why I ever come back here, you despicable people.' This was greeted with howls of laughter from Priapus and Penthesilea, and with chortles from Diogenes. Priapus got so carried away that he started leaping around the room naked and climbing over the furniture shouting, 'Despicable, despicable.' I have to say that I felt for Cornelia. She was the only sincere person in the room, and at that stage I had no opinions about the substance of what they were saying.

All this time, I had been listening in astonishment, and finally I could stay quiet no longer. I stood up to remind them of my presence and said, 'If you, the major beneficiaries of this system, can only see its defects and its faults, why then should anyone else believe in it?'

'Well said, young man!' Cornelia shouted.

'Frankly, I'm shocked,' I continued, 'and believe it an insult to everyone out there who is doing all they can to maintain our way of life.' Superbus, Nichilaeus and Diogenes looked very put out. Clearly my tiresome platitude required one of them to explain the abc of political argument.

It was Superbus, in his capacity as chairman, who spoke to me in a patient and didactic tone. 'Of course we are the major beneficiaries, but we are beyond the obligation to believe. This is one of the rights you earn with the Berlusconi Bonus – the right to criticise your own society. I admire your concern, but let me assure you that this is all harmless stuff. It is like listening to live music. We can do it – we few exceptional human beings can do it – but if everyone did it, then the system would eventually collapse. It is precisely because we ultimately respect our system that we would never approve of this kind of discourse in society as a whole.'

'Simply because you have the power?' I objected.

'What power? Who has power in our society? One of the most sophisticated aspects of our society – and I think that for once Nichilaeus and Diogenes will agree with me – is that it is very difficult to pinpoint exactly where power lies. In monarchical systems power clearly lay with the throne, in the Soviet Union power lay with the Politburo, but in our society the source of power is much more hidden, and hidden power is much more powerful and much more effective than identifiable power. Am I powerful? Are these people powerful? I think it would be more correct to say that we are free. I give a lot of money – a lot of money,' he repeated with a bitter laugh, 'to the New Liberty Party because such donations open up doors to interesting places, but I could just as easily give the money to the New Freedom Party and the same doors would be opened. This doesn't give me power; it doesn't even give me much influence, as there are plenty of BBs with open purses. It simply gives me access, but having gained access I am still a little uncertain as to where the real source of power lies.'

At this stage I realised that naked Penthesilea was seated on naked Priapus, facing towards him and leaping up and down on him very energetically, while he leered at us first from under one of her arms, then from under the other. 'Be like us,' he panted, 'do something useful!'

'Freedom,' she shouted, 'fuck for f-r-e-e-d-o-m.' Her voice rose to her highest pitch on the last word as a theatrical sign of her pleasure.

'These meetings are bad enough on the best of occasions,' said Cornelia, lifting herself and her towel to the full height of her dignity, 'but when Priapus comes along, they just descend into farce.' She left the baths without looking back.

'Good riddance, you useless hag,' howled Priapus with that schoolboy energy of his.

'Good riddance, bitch,' said Penthesilea more flatly.

Nichilaeus shook his head in knowing disdain, and everyone stood up to leave. The puffs of steam seemed unaffected by our own hot air, and I don't know what had been more enervating, our own convoluted exchanges or the warm damp air that drew sweat from every pore. We left the sexual athletes to their exercises, and Superbus muttered his disapproval to Nichilaeus. I had never previously met people who had such a good opinion of their own opinion, with the exception of Priapus who had not come to demonstrate the prowess of his brain. I had never seen sex whose purpose was to be a spectacle. As there is very little of the voyeur in me, I felt embarrassment, even shame, and not a little envy that people could be so confident about their bodies as to display themselves in that manner. I thought of my own overweight and ugly body, and realised how far my essence was from theirs. There was enough of the puritan in me to shudder at their promiscuity and enough of the time-conscious businessman to feel relief at not being such a slave to sexual instinct. Although I found the debaters completely incomprehensible, I had learnt several things from the debate. I now knew a little more about the Great Fukuyama's ideas, of which we heard little at school apart from the fact that he invented the End-of-History. I had learnt that people argue about things, even fiercely, not because they really care but because they get an intellectual pleasure from the process. But most importantly I had seen that the rich are more themselves than anyone else, and the freedom of wealth is overwhelming for most people. Poverty may grind you down and stop you from creating your own personality or potential, but wealth drowns you in a sea of choice and endless things you *could* be if only you had the hunger to become them. Wealth should be freedom, but often becomes imprisonment within a reality that puts up no resistance. Wealth isolates psychologically and intellectually. Wealth and dialogue are almost incompatible. Perhaps a society that ensured that everyone was above a certain threshold of poverty and below a certain threshold of wealth would not be such a bad idea after all.

When you work to become rich, when you work to make

something of your life, it is not always possible to develop your character and your ability to deal with others. I had few friends. My relationship with Constantia had been an emptiness from which we both withdrew. Or rather, we were both empty places that needed to be filled by the exuberance of more outgoing people. Our particular similarities made us incapable of providing company one to the other. When I met my fellow Berlusconi Bonuses, I felt they must have made their money by other, much easier means. For all their extraordinary differences and their restless desire to be more than themselves, they shared one important common characteristic: a complete familiarity with the business of being wealthy. I would probably have achieved this state with time and become harmless froth like those wealthy dabblers in ideas at the Turkish baths. But I was to meet intellectuals whose ideas were as hard as rocks and affect people's lives. I will leave it to others – to wiser minds than mine – to decide who was virtuous and who was not.

CHAPTER EIGHT

The Living Live Musician

I CAN'T SAY that I forgot about Younce, Linklater and Edith during that period leading up to my disturbing encounter with Younce. I tried to remove them from my conscious mind, but I was always aware of how each constituted a particular and related threat to the enjoyment of my new status. The night after my visit to the CSA building was one of terror and insomnia. I had now realised the magnitude of the random forces that had chosen me as their plaything. Younce was the reason I wanted to forget Edith, but now I knew he would not go away, I could not wait to see her. Incapable of sorting things out for myself, I instinctively turned to her as the person with whom I had an intimate relationship and, despite the fact she was uncarded, the person with whom I felt I had most in common. The next day, tired and unable to think clearly, but also strangely elated, I decided to do something very uncharacteristic – I decided to go and see her illegally, whatever the consequences. Of course, I had my BB, but then the business these people were in was beyond the BB. I reflected that a BB is supposed to put people beyond the law and confer upon them impunity and freedom from anxiety, but my BB had made me more constricted than before – and what is worse, more fearful.

I took a taxi as I had never learnt to drive. I failed the test at school and was never really interested. Since fuel prices soared, we don't use cars for long journeys but they remain very much part of our lifestyles and our economy. They are still the main indicator of status. But I was interested in other things: I was interested in bedpans, their disposable linings and, above all, their supply to as many Free Market Super-Saver Trust Hospitals as possible. Taxis are very expensive as drivers are only allowed to work for two hours a day, although this rule is not really enforced. The driver was silent for the entire journey, but his car wasn't. A television was showing a horse race from the history period, and the commentator's voice could just be heard, in spite of being turned down low and having to compete with a pop station on the radio. Occasionally the taxi-firm radio would crackle with an exchange of unintelligible messages. The last time I had taken this journey, Linklater had been lecturing me about this and that, and I had understood very little. Yet my trepidation and sense of unreality were greater on this second occasion. The noise generated in the vehicle's interior only served to increase my agitation and alienation. Once we had swung off the M25, I examined more carefully the string of gated communities between the motorway and the detention camp. They all flew their own corporate flags and vied with each other in their hybrid architectures. The range of building materials was vast – brick, aluminium and glass, reconstituted stone, wooden slatting, concrete – but their disparate styles were strangely uniform. Difference, it appears, cannot be generated artificially; true difference is random, and is the child of chaos and nature.

When I got to the Fukuyama, the man in the three-cornered

hat was as usual sitting morosely at the ticket office, and as I crossed the car park, he studied me with the patient stare of a man in no hurry to pass his day. 'Back again, are we? Now what could it be in this hellhole that attracts a smart city slicker like yourself?' He did not seem particularly interested in getting an answer. 'Ticket?'

'I haven't got one.'

'Well now, that could be a problem, but it so happens that today it isn't, because I'm feeling generous, there aren't many guards around and you haven't brought that arrogant fool Linklater with you.'

I had been prepared to wave my BB identity card in front of him, but I wasn't sure of its effect on this eccentric man. 'I'm looking for Edith.'

'Edith? Are we now? Well, you have got yourself in a flummox.'

'Do you know where she lives?' I insisted.

'Edith is a common name,' he remarked thoughtfully and unhurriedly.

'She wears a maid's uniform from the history period.'

'Maid's uniforms are nearly as common as three-cornered hats. Maids and highway robbers, that's the history the public liked best, when we still used to do the history bit in here.'

'Things must have been better then.'

'Well I don't know about that.' He gave this thought some consideration. 'My parents were still alive. My father was a wonderful singer, you know. He came from Russia – from a city called Nizhny Novgorod. Such a beautiful name, don't you think? Try saying that: Nizhny Novgorod.'

'Nizhny Novgorod.'

'Not bad. So much more beautiful than Basingstoke or Hatfield, don't you think?'

'I suppose so,' I said impatiently.

'He taught me Russian. There were a lot of Russians then – and Ukrainians, Georgians, Chechens, all sorts. My mother, on the other hand, was Nigerian. She too had a beautiful voice, but above all she was a great musician. You name an instrument and she could play it. You know I was born in this Fukuyama. I have spent my entire life here, but I believe that I know the world better than most people, better than you - and do you know why?'

'Why?' I asked dutifully.

'Because in those days there were people here from every corner of the globe. Everyone had their own story and as a child I would sit around with the adults and listen as they described the worlds, the many worlds they had left behind. Now they are all dead or have been integrated into the citizenry to fulfil the government's demographic targets.'

'Edith, the woman who hangs about with Linklater?'

He ignored my question and seemed to wince at the mention of Linklater. 'On the other hand, some things have improved. Thankfully we don't have to do any of that history stuff anymore. We were like performing monkeys.' He straightened and looked me proudly in the eye. 'My father, you know, was a surgeon, but not only that: he was a highly educated man. He loved literature, he loved history, he loved song, he loved company.' The man's eyes became a little watery and his expression indignant. 'And you know, every day he had to go out dressed up as a stupid gladiator and fight pretend fights with a heavily-built Nigerian dressed in a leopard skin. That Nigerian was my uncle and that's how my father met my mother. Can you think of a more humiliating life for two intelligent men, for…' He seemed overcome by emotion. 'At the time they called us economic migrants and bogus asylum-seekers. The West did all it could to ruin our countries, and then, when our parents were driven to these cold foreign shores by various mixtures of political repression and financial desperation, it locked them up in cesspits like this one.'

'Edith. I wanted to know about the woman called Edith.'

'I have always had a soft spot for fools, and a man who goes around the country calling for his Edith can only be considered a fool. So I have a soft spot for...'

I could see why Linklater hated this insolent man. 'If I am such a fool, how come I have a Berlusconi Bonus,' I interrupted him and held the opened identity card in front of his face. He looked at it for a few seconds with only a hint of surprise. 'And you, my friend, have never been able to get out of this cesspit,' I continued, now shaking with anger. 'It's not difficult to claw your way out of a Fukuyama these days, as we know how desperate they are for people.'

'So you're a BB and I'm a Fukuyama person. But does that mean that you have a better life. What do you do exactly?'

'I made my money supplying medicines to Hospital Trusts. I buy cheap and sell dear. That is the secret of our civilisation.'

'Very good,' he smiled triumphantly. 'Come with me.' He took me into a room behind the ticket office that no longer sold tickets. It appeared that it was all part of his house. Perhaps he had built the house around the ticket office. The room was large, whitewashed and well-lit. The walls were hung with a wide range of musical instruments. He took one down and started to play. I had never heard live music before and the sound appeared to vibrate off the walls with a warmth that cut straight through the iron logic of my RCI card and made me inexplicably want to cry from a strange and irrational kind of enjoyment. 'That's a violin,' he announced once he had stopped playing. He then took down a similar instrument: 'This one has been tuned as a fiddle.' He again started to play, but this time the music made me want to tap my toes. 'That is a jig. Countries near here that opted to stay in the European Union, called Ireland, Scotland and Wales, these countries produce a lot of music like that. Of course, you can hear such music in Kaylie Bars around the country, but it was all recorded in the history period. That is true of all music: pop, soul, blues, punk, jazz, classical, modern classical, all the categories that you will see in your malls, in your music shops - all that music was recorded in the history period. Do you know what that means?'

I uttered an exasperated 'no'.

'It means no singers, no musicians, no bands, no recording studios, no technicians, no copyrights, and above all no instruments and no instrument-makers. Come with me.' Again he was smiling warmly as he led me into another room. This was a long room with long workbenches and a great mass of tools. There were several musical instruments lying on the benches at various stages in the production process. The finished instruments in the other room had been beautiful, but these unfinished ones had a fascination all of their own. I could clearly see where each piece of wood neatly fitted into the whole, and felt a slight melancholy that they would not remain in their perfectly unfinished state for long. They laid bare their mysterious secrets, and that only increased my admiration for the hands that had formed them.

'Do you know why I hate Linklater?' the man asked.

'No.'

'Every so often other musicians in the Fukuyama come down here and we make music, many types of music, late into the night. Occasionally we allow a bunch of BBS to come and hear us play. You see this small pot of varnish. Do you know how much I have to pay for this? Twenty-five dollars. It has to be imported from India, you see. There is no call for varnish in a country where robotised factories produce everything in plastic or with plastic surfaces. You see all these tools for making instruments: every single one is imported. They cost a fortune.'

'So where do you get the money?'

'The BBs pay handsomely for the privilege of listening to a bit of live music. They get a kick out of doing something vaguely illicit, which of course is no problem for them. I'm sure they get up to some things that are really bad. They protect me from the police, and I get money and the opportunity to do what I like: making music and making musical instruments. I don't particularly like the BBs, but I don't hate them either. Some of them are quite interesting and are not as pro-regime as you might think. Others are just greedy for any experience life can give them – rather sad individuals without any direction.'

'And where does Linklater come into this?'

'He only goes and reports us all to the police, shouting from the hilltops that laws should apply to everyone in the same degree: BBs, ordinary citizens and Fukuyama people. Of course, it was like pissing in the wind. BBs can do almost anything, and they can certainly go and listen to as much illicit live music as they want. The authorities aren't that bothered as it takes place in a Fukuyama and doesn't involve ordinary citizens getting involved in productive activities; just a bunch of BBs listening to music produced by a few Fukuyama people. Of course, the police came down here a few times to check that all the citizens really had BBs and then went off bowing and scraping.'

'Linklater might have point. Maybe laws should be for everyone.'

'Don't give me that! Linklater comes down here with his superior attitudes and grand ideas, but what does he know about Fukuyamas. That's how we survive – by bending the rules. He wants to save the world – but have we asked to be saved? As far as I'm concerned, the damage has already been done. They've destroyed everything that was worthwhile, all I can do... all I want to do is create and recreate a little of the beauty that has disappeared. But I don't kid myself. What I do isn't a patch on what went before. As far as the instrument-making is concerned, I am practically self-taught, which inevitably means I could not have competed with people who in the history period were apprentices to apprentices to apprentices back over centuries, with everyone adding their own little touch of genius. That is history and that is what they have destroyed. Why bother with all this conspiracy stuff? Who is going to change things back? They couldn't, even if they wanted to.'

'Isn't that what the rebels call defeatism?'

'Is it defeatist to be realistic? Is it defeatist to ask, why risk so much suffering? People like Linklater would be fine if they were the only ones to pay for their ideas, but their ideas involve and ruin the lives of thousands of others, who otherwise would just continue their grumbling, humdrum but nevertheless meaningful lives, meaningful in their own small worlds.'

'Like your music.'

'If you like. But it's up to the individual to find a way round the absurd rules that society imposes on us and which society to some extent needs. It was the same in the history period.'

'So nothing has changed. Things are neither better nor worse. We are simply living the inevitable human condition.'

'No, things are worse, much worse. It's the scale of the thing, you see. In the time of history, empires rose and fell. They uprooted individuals, destroyed cultures, imposed religions, but they also generated interesting new hybrids, and in any case, they never had the entire globe in their hands. Now all the magnificent differences are disappearing: the music, the songs, the stories, the languages, they only survive in pallid commercialised forms. One of the problems with the decision of Ireland, Scotland and Wales to stay with the European Union is that it encouraged the Europeans to keep English as their official language: Euringlish, they call it now, but it is just English with a particularly Latinate vocabulary and a highly contorted syntax.

It is even flatter than Federation English, which is saying something. For the doubtful advantage of everybody being able to speak to everybody else in every part of their union (and you have to remember that nobody seems to say very much these days), they traded away their linguistic wealth, their wonderful tower of Babel.

'Even if the Linklaters of this world were to carry out their revolution and even if they wanted to revive the wonderful local intricacies that have been destroyed, which I think very unlikely, they would not be able to do it – not with the best will in the world. And they don't have the best will in the world – not people who go around with the answer to all the world's problems in their pockets. This guy Fukuyama also held the secrets of the world in his pocket, and look at this mess that is named after him. He sung the victory song of extreme free-market economics. Every emperor throughout history has had his court bard to celebrate his victories and assure him that his dynasty will reign forever, but this time the emperor was not a man but the Last Man: the idealised Western consumer. The Last Man, who Fukuyama despised and left prey to energetic entrepreneurs, the real inheritors of this earth, has no more chance of ruling forever than the emperors of the past. I am more bothered by the principal Fukuyamist slogan they teach at school, even here in these glorified detention camps: "We are building the Universal and Homogeneous State". Surely it is the chaos of our differences that keeps us alive. That is nature. That is the natural multiplication of variants: biological variants, linguistic variants, musical variants, cultural variants, each existing because of its differences and its similarities. Universal love is not the elimination of difference; it is man at peace and wonderment with the differences of his environment, the endless differences that are too many for us to know – should be too many for us to know. Any attempt to mould all mankind in our own image is not the Last Man, but man playing god. And that has always meant destruction. What is different now is that the destruction is irreversible. Nature may well be the ultimate victor, but the diversity of human society will be lost forever.'

'A gloomy picture,' I declared, now overwhelmed but not repulsed by the strange man's strangely convincing arguments. 'It's all so confusing and it's difficult for us citizens to get a handle on these things.'

'Of course, it's difficult because you have no language of thought and values. Modern society is not more complex, but its collective decisions have more far-reaching effects and therefore require more thought. It's ironic that when history developed more slowly, no one disputed its existence, though they still wanted to fight against it. Constancy was the ultimate aim for society and one of the greatest virtues for an individual. Now that all we see is the present, constancy counts for nothing. Now that we have banned history, we allow massive changes to take place without a moment's thought and we do not notice them. History, I believe, is moving fast and destroying what we might call the social mind that has evolved over millennia. Constancy is of little value in the immediacy of modern life, and yet constancy holds society together. Constancy is not conservatism; it is not blind and stupid tradition, but allegiance to the language of thought and values. Constancy is not an idea; it is the means of expressing an idea. If, say, I am constant in my love for my wife for forty years, my love is obviously completely different in its fortieth year from what it was in its first, but the means through which I express that love is the same because it is part of an unbroken chain of feelings and thoughts. A marriage is a micro-culture. Now, if this is true of an individual's passion, then it is even truer of a society's culture across the generations.'

He stopped talking, looked at me and started to laugh. 'You'll think I'm worse than Linklater if I go on much longer. Well, every now and then, you have to blast off a few opinions, but little good it does you beyond the pleasure of the outburst itself. The girl you're looking for is called the Mass's Edith, after her mother who we call the Mass.'

'Why the Mass?'

'Because she is enormously fat.'

'That's not very socially correct', I objected.

'No, we're not very SC in here. Your ever-so-SC authorities do not register our surnames at birth because they don't want us to have any genealogy. They want us to be all present and no history, but of course we insist on relating everyone to their parents by our own system of nicknames.'

'Where does she live?'

'That I couldn't tell you, but if you find the Mass, then you'll find Edith. The Mass keeps a tearoom in the little square you reach straight down from this entrance. It is only frequented by policemen, spies and subversives, because no self-respecting Fukuyama person would drink the Mass's hellish tea and coffee. Outsiders think we have no taste because we have no money, but we think citizens have no taste because those RCI cards kill off any discernment in the brain. It strikes me that an RCI card measures price for quantity but the computer-programmers who designed it forgot to factor in quality.'

'I noticed that her coffee was rather disgusting,' I said defensively.

'Then you are a man of discernment,' he hugged me with one arm, 'at least for a citizen. Listen, there are many rumours about Edith. You seem a nice young man, so be careful. They say she is a dangerous woman. They say...' With his arm still round my back he turned his head to look at me, and then, as if remembering that he knew nothing about me, he withdrew and a cautious diffidence descended on him. He wore his new expression awkwardly because it was not in his nature to hold aloof. 'No. I shouldn't add gossip to gossip. People say a lot of things, and little of it is true. I'm sure she's a perfectly ordinary young woman.'

Perhaps, if he had told me what I am now sure he was going to tell me, I might now be sitting in the Berlusconi Bonus Club drinking a gin and tonic, rather than sitting in a cell writing my 'confession'. But then again, such is the folly of love, even in the case of a man with an RCI Card buried deep in his brain, that I might have ignored his advice, I might have become indignantly angry, I might have thanked him by punching him in the face. There is little point in dwelling on these things. He did not tell me what he knew and I set off to find the Mass.

CHAPTER NINE

Withholding from Edith

THE MASS WAS sitting in dismal solitude. When I asked her where Edith was, she didn't answer but instead started to move. It was a difficult process, and a few seconds passed before I realised that she actually wanted to stand up. I thought that perhaps I should give her a hand, but decided not to for two reasons. Firstly, it might have been rude and, secondly, I have to confess that I found her repulsive. This entirely irrational prejudice may have been produced by my Rational Consumer Implant card. Citizens are by no means all sylph-like, myself included, and many are far more obese than the Mass, but I'm told that the RCI card has the thinness drive programmed into it. Therefore we all feel terribly upset about our fatness and go out to spend fortunes on vain attempts to get thin, except of course for that minority of our population who spend their entire time running marathons, drinking carrot juice and becoming ill through a lack of calories. This woman, on the other hand, appeared disgustingly at ease with her fatness. Indeed I would say that she was entirely beyond desire.

She struggled along at a snail's pace but without any protest. After turning into several narrow alleys smelling of bad plumbing, we came to one where she stopped and uttered the only words I ever heard pass her lips: 'yellow door.' Those words were sufficient for me to detect a heavy foreign accent. I realised that whatever language the Mass was thinking in, it was not English, and I believe that in her mind she kept alive a land that was not England.

Edith's house was different from the others: cleaner, and the door and windows had been recently painted in a garish yellow. I entered and found myself in a room that was both cluttered and tidy, by which I mean there was far too much stuff, and it was all new, polished, dusted and carefully set out. Edith jumped out a chair and rushed over to embrace me. As I have said, a man in love believes what he wants to believe, and I enjoyed the closeness of her body and the warmth of her greeting. I enjoyed our lovemaking upstairs, and was not too upset when immediately afterwards she lit a cigarette and said in a very matter-of-fact voice, 'Adolphus, we must talk business.'

It was back to the infinitely complex geometry between myself, Linklater, Younce and Edith. It made my head ache. That was the moment in which I felt most acutely aware of being put upon, a feeling that had dogged me since the whole affair began. I didn't care about changing the world, but neither did I care about keeping it as it was. I was not driven by any desire to attain moral superiority by saving humanity from itself, because it is itself and I knew and still know that there is almost nothing I can do to change it or to stop it from changing. There are a few men and even fewer women who can change the world on a grand scale; very rarely are these persons morally superior to us more circumscribed individuals, although they mostly claim to be. I have my own little life; it is short and probably pretty insignificant; to pass it in the most pleasant way possible had been my mundane ambition. Some might say that this was not only a selfish ambition, which it clearly was, but also an extravagant one. That may be the case, if we consider the realities of human existence, a pastime that Linklater and Younce find so consuming, but it was a small ambition if we consider that it is shared by the great majority of those who experience human existence. It was extravagant in its modesty.

What did I care about? In that particular moment, I cared about Edith's innocent blue eyes, her perfectly straight but not pointed nose, her thin but not overly thin lips and her yellow-blond hair which she wore short and spiky. Hers is a beautiful face, a little sharp but still beautiful. Of course, if you took an objective look at all the various physiognomies in the world, you might find that the European one looks a little mean. And Edith's very European face is a little mean: it seems to say 'I am alone, I don't understand the world and I don't trust it'. Hence the mixture of innocence and aggression that rationally I should have distrusted, but in fact found heart-stoppingly attractive. I sometimes think that my RCI card was faulty or that they put it in upside down. It certainly did not appear to work very well. I was always a grafter in one of the last and most important activities left open to us: the buying and selling of goods. I was never a very passionate consumer, and still less am I a man devoid of passions. The invisibility of those passions to everyone around me and indeed sometimes to myself only shows how inept we are at distinguishing between the sincere and the synthetic.

'We have a spy in our midst,' she announced, immediately striking me with terror. I was the spy – or was I? 'Don't worry, I am not accusing you. This spy has been around for a long time, and I think I know who he is.'

'Who?' I was obliged to say by her pause, so typical of our spy games, our bluffs and double-bluffs – so typical of the rhetoric they used to lead me into the morass.

'Linklater.'

'That's ridiculous.' Now I do not claim to be a great judge of character, but neither am I wholly bereft of some instinctive sense that judges people without necessarily analysing them. Linklater might have been many things, but I could not have thought of him as a spy. At that time I did not find him an attractive personality, but I did believe him to be sincere. Indeed it was precisely that sincerity that made me distrust him, because it seemed to be coupled with excessive self-belief. Later, I realised that my bad opinion of him was based on what I then considered the outlandishness of his beliefs.

'I too could not believe it, and it took me some time to realise the truth. It has to be someone in a very central position, as the authorities know everything we do before we do it. I am of the opinion that Linklater is at the centre of an enormous network of spies that is impeding the whole liberation movement, and without liberation in the West, there's no chance of it anywhere else, because all the military power is here.'

These arguments always leave me cold. They are so categorical and they are often used to slip away from the main argument – in this case whether or not Linklater was a spy. My instincts told me he definitely was not. 'So what are we going to do about it?' I asked.

'We're going to carry out an action that Linklater knows nothing about and we're going to hit the enemy hard. We're going to blow up...'

'I don't like the sound of "blow up". You can count me out if you're going to blow anything up.'

'Linklater is always saying we must hit their economy, but what do we do? We make pointless attempts at liaising between different Fukuyamas.'

It never occurred to me at the time that the reason why our own attempt to liaise between two Fukuyamas had failed was that we made the unilateral decision to engage in entirely different activities of a personal nature. 'We are going to blow up a railway line,' she continued. 'We'll hit one of the main arteries of their whole system for shifting goods from robotised factories to the main consumer centres.' She seemed very determined.

'But what about the trains?'

'We'll be doing it in the middle of the night, stupid.'

Why was I arguing? I would have to inform Younce. 'Alright, I take your point. Keep me informed. I think I should be going,' I turned to go, even more troubled than I had been before my visit to Edith.

'Oh great,' she said. 'You really know how to give a woman a good time. Why don't we do something together? Why don't we go to a mall?'

I don't know why I've never really liked the malls. They have everything that involves the exchange of money and has sufficient consumer demand, so as a card-inserted citizen I should find their allure difficult to overcome. Besides the enormous range of shops, they have restaurants, cinemas, gyms, swimming pools and saunas, and yet the restaurants sell synthetic food, the cinemas sell revenge movies or hopelessly sentimental tripe that ends in a happy couple being happy somewhere (in spite of our astronomic divorce rates), the gyms are full of grunting men and women trussed up in muscles that look as though they're going to snap, the saunas are full of fat people sweating misery and the swimming pools are full of screaming children splashing each other in a manic and hyperactive manner. The thing I really hate about these manufactured paradises, built from the same modular units all over the Federation, is that they are sealed over with a transparent dome that maintains a steady temperature and saves you from getting wet when moving between buildings or carrying your shopping out to the car. You need never encounter unprocessed air on the trip from your integrated garage to the mall car park. .

'But what about your clothes?' I asked.

'I wasn't thinking of going out dressed up as a maid from the history period,' she answered with some irritation.

'And your papers? What if the guards ask for your papers?' I continued to parry. It wasn't just my antipathy for malls that disinclined me; it was also the idea of being in a mall with all my current preoccupations. It was not the moment.

'For fuck's sake, you're a BB,' her exasperation clearly showing; 'you can do any damn thing.'

'I know, but I can see no point in breaking the law for the sake of it,' I uttered while fully realising the complete inconsistency of my argument. Inconsistent, true enough, but consistent with my character which has always been innately law-abiding.

She jumped out of her seat, unsure whether to laugh or scream at me. 'Why the fuck did you become a BB? Why gain a privilege that allows you to break the law, if you have no desire to break the law?' Then her expression changed from mocking to suspicious: 'Why did you want to become a BB? I hope I haven't been fucking some perv. But then again, you don't strike me as the sort. You're odd, but not that kind of odd.'

'You're right,' I said, 'it is odd to want to be a BB if you don't want to make use of the right to break the law, but I was driven by a simple desire to make wealth and to display my success by obtaining a BB. Of course I broke the odd law and cheated on the tax, but I now know that that was nothing compared with what my fellow BBs got up to. I became rich by playing the market, and the Free Market Super-Saver Trust Hospitals overpay on almost everything to ensure a profit for their suppliers; so if a supplier comes along who wants to put in a few hours studying the market, then the profits can be astronomical. I never gave much thought to what I would do with a Berlusconi Bonus.'

'You never gave much thought,' she said incredulously. 'You

never gave much thought about something that lifts you up above everyone else. Christ, being a citizen wasn't enough for you. Going to the mall and spending your money wasn't enough for you. Why? What were you so greedy for? If you had no need of a BB, why didn't you get out and have some fun? Did you have a girlfriend while you were working so hard?'

'I did. She was called Constantia. Ours was not a passionate affair and it didn't last. She was completely unable to decide where she wanted to go. She lacked self-confidence, but in her dreams she wanted someone more outgoing than myself, someone with a more aggressive character, someone with more...'

'... more get-up-and-go. I can understand that,' she was now seated, relaxed and coldly detached.

'She never believed I would get a BB,' I ignored her remark and fought back with the one thing that distinguished me.

'So she must be really miffed to know you've got one now.'

'I don't know that Constantia was that kind of woman.'

'Still carry the torch, do we? Come on, what kind of woman? Do you understand women after one passionless affair? Why didn't you get out and have some fun? You citizens don't know you're born. Do you realise what a small a percentage of the world population you are – most of the world population lives in misery and you don't even know how to enjoy life in the midst of plenty – a plenty that is supposedly ruining the planet? Do you have any idea? Why didn't you get out and have some fun?'

I disliked the tone, but accepted it from her. 'Sex was never the thing that most interested me,' I replied.

'I kind of guessed that,' she sneered as she looked in her powder compact for spots on her perfect skin.

'I wanted a relationship,' I continued; 'I now understand why the relationship with Constantia didn't work or didn't work for me. As I said, it lacked passion, and now I know what passion is, because passion is what I feel for you, Edith.'

'Oh yeah!'

'Edith, I'm completely smitten.'

'But not enough to take me to the mall for lunch.'

'Edith, we have bigger problems. Another time.'

She took her time and patted her cheeks with a slight dusting of powder. She then snapped the compact shut and swung round towards me. 'Adolphus, that's enough for today. I'm off to see what joys can be found in this delightful detention camp that your civilisation sees fit to lock me up in. I'll be in touch.'

I took out my mobile to call a taxi, but she clearly wanted to express her impatience more forcefully. She moved across the room and taking me firmly by the elbow guided but did not push me out of the house. 'Call from the street; I have things to do.'

Edith's compact said much about her. No female citizens use compacts these days. The paraphernalia of make-up has grown much more complex and handbags are never large enough. Although I had never learnt to read the subtle language of consumer articles whereby a millimetre more fabric can transform a dress from jumble into high fashion and the colour of your mobile phone describes your character, I was aware that the old-fashioned compact showed that Edith was still very much a Fukuyama girl, in spite of her airs. Everything about her, including her frostiness, conspired to make me love her. And I had now declared my passion. I was out of my depth, and how could I inform on Edith?

CHAPTER TEN

The Sophist

I DECIDED ON a compromise. I would inform Younce that an attack was going to take place, but I would not give him any names. Besides I knew nothing about the location of the attack. I rang him on a special number he had given me and told him there would be an attack on a railway line, but to my surprise he asked me nothing about who was involved and nothing about where it was going to take place. 'Hibbert, this may sound strange, but I am going to have to ask you to go ahead with this action. We need to let them come out into the open. We need to see who they are. When is this terrorist outrage going to take place?' I told him that it would be in about a week's time, and he told me that he had set up my meeting with Michael Foxtrotter that evening. He gave me the address and rang off.

Foxtrotter has a spacious flat at the university overlooking a handsome quad. He greeted me unhurriedly and rather coldly, and took me through to his study. It too was lined with books. The desk in the middle of the room, although not as big as Younce's, was intricately carved and made of exquisite wood.

'Indian,' said Foxtrotter, noting my interest. 'Please sit down.' He waved his hand laconically towards the chair. 'Captain Hieronymus Younce has asked me to give you a little talk, because he feels that your situation, of which I know nothing and, I hasten to add, wish to know nothing, could expose you to irresponsible and dangerous ideas. As a businessman... as a citizen engaged in the natural pursuit of wealth and happiness, you will have had little experience of the anti-social elements that you are now encountering. I have no doubt of that.' Foxtrotter was a thickset man of medium height, and wore a pair of fashionable reading glasses. He appeared to be an aggressive man who had somehow cultivated an air of detached wisdom that sat oddly with his heavy muscular build, piercing eyes and near-white hair cut to a short stubble. He walked with the spring of the well-fed, well-exercised and well-thought-of.

'I want to start by telling you about history,' he spoke as someone who had delivered this lesson on previous occasions. 'I have no intention of discussing particular events, of course; that would only confuse you even more. Once you leave the world of business, which is quintessentially a world of the present, you constantly come up against history: it is what makes us what we are. A highly evolved society like the one we are lucky enough to live in now is the product of a long evolutionary process, in which humanity has had to fight off all manner of absurd distortions and superficially attractive ideologies. Now I am extremely critical of the current government line, so you can believe me when I say that they are absolutely right to keep history away from the consuming masses. History is strictly for the professional; in the hands of the non-professional it becomes a highly volatile substance. The twentieth century was marred by a series of man-made calamities caused by misplaced ideas that can be traced to historical myth.

'We have defeated history – an act of supreme will – by

embracing immediacy, flexibility and adaptability. We say and our politicians constantly repeat, "We are ruling nothing in and we are ruling nothing out." But in reality we quite wisely rule most things out; we rule out peace, public ownership, redistribution of wealth, taxation of the rich, and open markets for poor countries. So what does our flexibility consist of?' he asked with the professorial contentment of not expecting an answer. 'It consists of our rhetoric. The same politician may one day call himself a liberal, the next day a Christian, the day after a Third-Worlder wishing to defeat world poverty, and the day after that for particularly dramatic effect, a socialist. There was a prime minister in the history period called Tony Blair who was a trailblazer in this technique which makes it impossible to bring about change or even discuss change, because there can be no political debate when every political term means everything and therefore nothing. The sophists destroyed ancient democracy by skilfully making the weaker arguments appear the stronger, whereas Blair's technique was more straightforward but, in a way, more subtle: he bombarded voters with statistics, accurate yet also imaginative statistics that used such methodologies as double-accounting, triple accounting and, if someone in the electorate was still awake, quadruple accounting. This cut the demos out of democracy, a highly commendable aim. Blair was also famous for his sophisticated use of the glaring *non sequitur* to which a politician must cling limpet-like with an expression of unassailable moral superiority. Our own government very adeptly implemented this method in the recent war in Pakistan, Operation Extending Democracy and Justice. The newly established democracy had voted in Tassaduq Chengiz as their prime minister and this demagogue wanted to provide state education and health – with *no* international tenders. On top of that,' Foxtrotter's eyes spun to the ceiling to emphasise the absurdity of it, 'he wanted to nationalise the railways. Our president declared war on the basis that one of Chengiz's generals had a book on nuclear warfare in his library. Now anyone who is in the know knows full well that the general in question had been appointed by the previous military dictatorship with which we had excellent relations. A book on nuclear warfare is the kind of thing you might expect to find on a general's bookshelf and in no way proves an *intent* to develop weapons of mass destruction at some unspecified date in the future. Moreover we specialists also know that Pakistan did once have a nuclear capability but had to relinquish it in exchange for lifting sanctions imposed not only by the Federation but also by its powerful neighbour, India. Since then there has been a rigorous system of weapons inspection. None of this detracts from the essential fact that we must maintain the free exchange of goods and services across the globe, but such arguments are so prosaic. A country needs more heroic explanations of its behaviour, and the tried and tested *non sequitur* is still needed to clarify everything for the poor non-specialist who has to choose which party to vote for.' I was wondering why Younce had thought this would be useful for me: I couldn't understand a word the academic and official dissident was saying.

'It is true,' Foxtrotter adopted the air of a man about to deliver a well-pondered concession, 'that the establishment itself has slightly distorted Fukuyama's idea that we have reached the end of history. It has taken it a little too literally, as what we might say is that minor history continues, while major history, that is the history of ideology and the organisation of society, has indeed come to an end. We have now evolved a social organisation as perfectly suited to our natures in the civilised context as the hunter-gatherer society was suited to them in the uncivilised context.'

Foxtrotter paused to consider the effect of his words and see if I had any questions. I had none.

'The great merit of our society,' he continued, 'is that it creates perfect choice, or rather attempts to create perfect choice, which is not easy in a world that does not understand the meaning of the word "equality".'

'Equality?'

'Yes, equality,' he smiled. 'Another banned word, but I thought you might have come across it since you started working for Captain Younce, as a lot of subversives use this word in a very loose and misleading way. They say that we must do something about the Third World, and indeed we do spend billions of our hard-earned wealth attempting to re-establish order in these countries. But these subversives mean something else: they would like us to subsidise poor countries, because in their view such countries are too poor to trade themselves out of their difficulties. This is a profound misunderstanding of what equality means in the market place.' He then slowed his speech to emphasise that he had reached the most essential part of his lecture. 'Equality in the market place is the most important, indeed the only true form of equality, and essentially it is equality of opportunity. Why should we deprive these countries and their citizens of the dignity of fair competition? If they work hard and keep their noses clean, there is no reason why they shouldn't one day aspire to the standard of living we enjoy here. They are, in any case, the beneficiaries of the "trickle-down" effect from our own vibrant economies, although they never give us any credit for it. Equality is the very basis of our society, but unfortunately we cannot use the term in public discourse, because it is so open to irresponsible misinterpretation.'

He paused again and then said rather truculently, 'Do you not have any questions?'

It all seemed incomprehensible to me, but one element in his talk did ask for clarification. 'You said that you are a critic of this government. What,' I inquired, 'is the nature of your criticism?'

He looked at me contemptuously and expanded himself to the heights of his intellectual superiority. 'In what ways am I a critic of this regime? Well,' he chuckled to himself, 'the list is too long to enumerate. But I will give you one example since you ask. This government is far too lax with the European Union, which only really responds to threats. I know from years of experience and observation of political events that the EU is quite beyond rational discourse. Take, for instance, their obstinate refusal to make RCI cards obligatory for all citizens. Is this a level playing field? We have perfectly rational consumers buying European goods, while their irrational consumers often reject ours for entirely spurious reasons. We should take the matter to the WTO; we should threaten sanctions. Why isn't our government sticking up for the ordinary citizen of the Federation of Free Democratic States? Then there is the EU refusal to expel Muslims, when it is clear that their religion is quite incompatible with the proper functioning of a free market. Nor could you ever expect Islam to take on the subtleties of transcendental trading. So the poor citizen of the Federation is again put at a disadvantage in order to pander to European liberal sensitivities. This is what I mean by inequality! How can there be equality and a level playing field if some of their citizens are acting as irrational consumers and others are practising bizarre religions?'

His face was now red with anger, but he hadn't finished: 'Then there is their spineless approach to international affairs. In the Security Council, the European Union voted against five of our six most recent military interventions in the Third World. We citizens of the Federation of Free Democratic States bear the entire cost of policing this world, and they don't even give us moral support. They continually indulge in this tiresome anti-Federationism. They are quite incapable of understanding things as they really are. You know, I never eat courgettes or zucchini; I only eat liberty marrowettes. That's how strongly I feel about this whole question, including our government's criminal inaction. Some of these puerile anti-Federationists complain that not only do we rig the international system in our favour, but every time a Third-World country takes an independent line that harms Western interests we organise a coup or invade to set up our own puppet regime. Are they suggesting that we don't have a right to engage in quite legitimate off-balance-sheet activities? Do they think that after having invested massively in assets to protect the Free World, we don't have a right, or indeed a duty to use those assets? Since Fukuyama has discovered the true desirous, passive and economically selfish nature of the Last Man, we cannot entertain the possibility of other countries and other cultures coming up with rival definitions of the Last Man or any other kind of Man, which would be tantamount to restarting History. Fukuyama amusingly likened history to a wagon train trekking across the prairie to a town where history is ended,' Foxtrotter smiled knowingly. 'Each society is a wagon and some wagons are faster than others. Some are lost along the way and some are attacked by Indians. It is the duty of dissidents in the name of humanity to make sure that all societies have a chance to reach the End-of-History, and that is why we support all military interventions in the Third World.'

He stopped talking, almost exhausted by his diatribe, and started to drum his fingers on the desk as though undecided about what to do next. 'I suppose I could also touch on the territorial question, although it will be a bit too historical for you,' he said grudgingly. 'I have already mentioned Prime Minister Blair and how he invented "constructive opposition" – the brilliant idea of not attacking the policies of the government of the day, but taking them over and wrapping them up in an entirely new rhetoric. He also acknowledged the sacred role of the United States, which was to be the foundation on which the Federation of Free Democratic States was built. However, he made one terrible mistake, for which we are still paying some fifty years later: he gave limited autonomy to Scotland and Wales. He compounded his error by allowing them to introduce electoral systems that actually reflected the views of the electorate: an uncharacteristically reckless concession. This was surprising because Blair understood, just as we understand today, that only the powerful are supposed to govern: that is the first rule of meritocracy. And who defines merit, if not the powerful? When the Federation of Free Democratic States was established and a later New Labour government decided to leave the EU to join it, Scotland and Wales held referendums. The results were in favour of continued membership of the EU, and we lost those countries in the ensuing constitutional crisis. Of course, the Federation of Free Democratic States still disputes the losses.'

Suddenly I could see a possible entrée into this obscure conversation, using the information provided by the man in the three-cornered hat: 'Not only did we lose these territories, but Europe lost its linguistic variety, because now they speak Euringlish.'

'So? And what's wrong with that?' – he looked at me in confusion – 'although I agree that their type of English is pretty horrendous.'

'Well, isn't it a shame that all those beautiful languages have disappeared, only to be replaced by an ersatz one?' I continued, a little unsure of my ground.

Foxtrotter became visibly agitated and threw his glasses on the table to express his anger. His fierce eyes became fiercer and he rubbed his reddening forehead as though my hopelessly irresponsible words had caused him a headache: 'Who have you been talking to? I demand to know the source of this sedition!'

Stranger as I was to political discourse, I found his behaviour inexplicable, but I realised I had to protect the man in the three-cornered hat, who I had come to like. I thought of him in his workshop fashioning those elegant instruments that lack experienced players. I thought of the wonderful creative futility of it all. One day the BBS would grow tired of protecting him, and then the police would come and smash the instruments, the tools, the workshop. There can be no question of upsetting the market with unreliable investments in human creativity, when there is a ton of stuff from the history period that can be recycled for the rest of time. 'I was told of it by some fellow BBS,' I said.

'You lot never tire of playing at a little bit of this and a little bit of that. You must apprise Captain Younce of every detail,' Foxtrotter told me severely. 'I realise that this is going way over your head, but you must consider the dangers inherent in Europeans' speaking any language other than English – just think how it would skew the market. How would we sell our cultural products to Europe? Besides,' he added smugly, 'it gives us a certain intellectual advantage. We should never forget that.'

It seems that Captain Younce made a mistake in sending me to Foxtrotter. Most of what this official dissident passed way over my head, as he himself had predicted. But through the fog of his argument I began to understand that perhaps we humans really had lost something invaluable in recent history and that the man in the three-cornered hat, living in a concrete-block shack and never leaving what amounted to a detention centre, had keener perceptions than I or Michael Foxtrotter would ever have.

'Remember,' said Foxtrotter as he showed me out the door, 'if you work for Captain Younce, you are there to be his eyes and ears, and it is for him, not you, to process any information you pick up. Once the job has been completed, you can go and enjoy your BB, and forget all about history and equality.' As I left his flat little the wiser, I felt that the subversives seemed preferable as human beings to the anti-subversives.

CHAPTER ELEVEN

Discarding the Card

IT SEEMED INCREASINGLY likely that Linklater really was the spy. The situation was becoming very complex, murky even. The whole thing really was like one of those thrillers from the history period. I now know that thrillers are much to be preferred on the screen or between the covers of a book than as a reality to be lived. Who was betraying whom? Well, for starters, I was betraying both sides to some extent, not to fulfil some extravagant conspiratorial plan, but because I felt mixed loyalties. That was the really scary thing: I had no plan and was incapable of even starting to formulate one.

Linklater was certainly an unconvincing subversive. Even I could see that he said too much and trusted too much. It made much more sense that Edith would want to overturn the regime, as she owed it nothing. Linklater must have been fairly affluent, even though it was difficult to see where he spent his money. It is, however, impossible to practice law in England or anywhere else in the Federation without making a great deal of wealth. It occurred to me that Linklater might be an *agent provocateur*, who recruited possible malcontents so that Captain Younce could keep an eye on them.

Given these reflections of mine, I felt a little embarrassed when Linklater rang and asked me to meet him at his home immediately. He greeted me warmly and quickly ushered me into his study. There was something very disarming about his muddled and stooping manner. There was a desk in the middle of his study. It was considerably smaller than Younce's and Foxtrotter's, but made of the same exquisite wood. It was also much less ornate, although in its understated way it was perhaps the most beautiful.

'Indian,' he said, as I openly admired it. 'Anything of any worth these days is made in India. Anything that requires skill is made there. You see their entire population is uncarded. All the western economies are now carded or partially carded, the Third World including China is in a state of anarchy, and India alone retains a mixed economy with a well-functioning education system. They provide skilled personnel and luxury goods to the West. As you know that the Federation has been cutting down on trades and professions for many years. There are no tradesmen now, and there are no artists, musicians or writers. We rely on India to supply those skills we lack. Once the cyclical newspaper system has been perfected, there will be no more journalists. The RCI cards produce a purely consumer society. I don't know why they have this bizarre idea that it is consumption that brings happiness. Human beings actually enjoy a time-gap between their desire for something and their realisation of it. That's why production is so much more likely to bring contentment. True, the industrial production of the twentieth century was alienating, but creative production is what humans love most. With consumption, gratification is immediate and gratification inevitably has a measure of disappointment. With production, on the other hand, gratification is anticipated and that anticipation engages with the perfect idea of the desired object. On completion, production obviously has its own disappointments, but as there is a degree of personal control, it also provides information on how the object could be better produced in the future.'

'You can be sure of this?' I interrupted, now a little bored of being lectured at, although Linklater was the only one of my lecturers who was not intimidating.

'Can we be sure of anything?' he replied merrily. 'But take a look at this!' He threw a newspaper at me and intimated that I should read it. It was called *The Euringlish Times*. Immediately under that masthead there was a message written in a polite and didactic tone, but the English was obscure and very foreign sounding: 'The very gentle readers are begged to deposit their newspapers, once they have read them, in the apposite litter containers installed in our cities in accordance with Legislative Decree No. 246 of 19 March 2048. Your fellow citizens will thank you for your remarkable gentleness. Remember that a clean city is more beautiful.' I noted that in Europe they still counted the years. I wondered how long it would be before they progressed to the enlightened system of only recording days and months.

'At the bottom of the page: the bit about RCI cards,' Linklater urged.

'Ah, you mean this bit,' and I started to read, '"The European Union has accorded today that by March 2055, it will have rendered obligatory for all EU citizenry to be implanted with international standard RCI cards. The EU Minister of the Interior Gianni Paglia issued the following declaration «Certain people have argued that at this moment in time the EU is obligated to adopt an independent position. I respect their point of view. We always need a fortified Europe but Europe is much more fortified when it collaborates with the Federation of Free Democratic

States, and we reject the puerile anti-Federationism which is again preponderating here in the EU.» The minister also added that the EU will not be withdrawing its 30-man contingent from the Federation-led coalition in Malaysia, but will be keeping them there until the Malaysians are ready for democratic elections next year."'

'The Federation has put so much pressure on them that they have finally buckled,' Linklater commented. 'This is a dark day for humanity and for our struggle. Europe is currently our main source of radical publications. The movement is far stronger over there.'

'So what's so wrong with an RCI card?' I asked a little testily. 'We all have one, after all.'

'Well, I don't,' he replied beaming, and then lowering his head he parted his hair to reveal inexpert stitches on the top of his cranium; 'I removed it long ago, and before the night's out, I would like yours to be removed too.'

'Hold on, a moment,' I protested; 'not only is that highly illegal, but I'll have you know that my RCI card never stopped me from being very successful.'

'It is precisely because you have achieved so much in spite of having your RCI card that I have chosen you for a special task. I know that Younce has recruited you; you as good as told me so, but it is your honesty that makes me think I can trust you. And I can trust you, can't I?'

'I don't know,' I hesitated. 'You might be a spy!'

He laughed. 'Adolphus, my friend, if I were a spy, I wouldn't bother with reading so many books, would I now? I would just learn a little pseudo-revolutionary jargon at spy school, and trot it out when required.'

'I don't know about that. Captain Younce has a study full of books, and he is the spy chief.'

'Exactly, he is the spy chief and not a spy. He reads the books because he really has to understand people like me. You know, I often feel that Younce is a lot like me, but the image is inverted, as in a mirror. We both love ideas above all other things. He reads my favourite books in order to understand me, and I read his favourite books in order to understand him. He works for the powerful, I for the powerless. He believes in the rule of men, and I in the rule of laws. He believes that order is a product of homogeneity; I believe that homogeneity will destroy humanity. But for some inexplicable reason, I respect Younce. I know that he will destroy me, because he has all the cards in his hands. We cannot possibly win in the short term, and yet this society will destroy itself unless we can persuade the establishment to change course. I know that Younce is a ruthless man, but he is also an intelligent one. Eventually men like him will have to realise the futility of the ideology they so fiercely protect. In the meantime, all we can do is sharpen our arguments and attempt to open as many channels of dialogue as possible.'

At that moment, his doorbell rang and he pleaded, 'Will you have your card removed?'

'I don't know. That would put me firmly on the side of the subversives.'

'Precisely, that's another reason why you have to have it done,' he went to the door and let in two men. I could see they were Fukuyama people even though they weren't wearing history clothes. They had a weary and ill-fed look, which was exacerbated by their obvious nervousness about being in the area without proper papers.

The two men looked at me and my uncertainty, and then one of them said to Linklater, 'I hope we haven't made this trip for no reason.' I am not keen on making sudden decisions, but I realised that time was not on my side. I thought of Younce and Foxtrotter on one side and Edith and Linklater on the other, and I clearly preferred the latter two, whatever differences or misunderstandings there might have been between them. 'Okay,' I muttered. The men picked me up bodily and laid me down on the sofa. One of them immediately applied a local anaesthetic. Hardly waiting for it to take effect, the other started to open up the top of my cranium. In no time, stitches were applied, the men were out the door, and a bloody RCI card lay on the floor.

From that moment, I was deprived of the technological prop that guides one's thoughts towards rational self-interest. My emotions, far from being purer, were now more contradictory, one could even say more muddied and depressingly obscure. I can see why the regime sings the praises of consumer society and RCI cards, because my liberation did not lighten my soul, it weighed it down. I think that of all the emotions that flooded into my mind, compassion was the heaviest and most troublesome, because it set off my thoughts in so many conflicting directions. Nevertheless, having the card removed was a liberation, and I have no regrets. As I write these provocative notes, this senseless and dangerous confession, itself the futile act of an uncarded man, I treasure the short period of my life in which I became what nature intended me to be: a human being who thinks and acts like a human being.

CHAPTER TWELVE

Linklater Puts His Trust In Me

FOLLOWING MY MINOR operation, I must have fallen asleep on Linklater's sofa. The next thing I saw was him standing over me and offering me a cup of coffee. His tall and stooping body was set against the plain ceiling, and his unfocused eyes, oval face and thin lips smiled at me with benign, almost paternal condescension. Only a fool could not have grasped the man's profound honesty, but I have often been a fool and now my foolishness haunts me and compels me to commit this desperate act.

'How are you feeling?' he asked kindly as I sat up and he handed me the cup. 'We need to talk.'

I stood up in my crumpled clothes and walked across to a table where he was already sitting down and tidying up scattered newspapers and books.

'I need to explain a few things to you, Adolphus,' he deliberated, although still retaining his friendly and confidential air. 'I want to assure you that I have no blueprint, no master plan, no off-the-shelf utopia that will put all things right. Firstly, there would be little point, given that even our most modest objectives have little chance of success at the moment. Secondly, I don't believe in such things anyway. Society is so complex that any easy answers must be viewed with suspicion. Fukuyama's end-of-history is also referred to as the end of ideology, but in fact it was the victory of one extreme ideology over another, and he sang the victory anthem. All ideologies reduce individuals to a Perfect Man who acts as an ideal man would if not interfered with by the imperfections of history. Fukuyama believed that man as created by liberal democracy is governed by economic self-interest, although some continue to be influenced by what he called *thymos*, the desire for recognition.'

'I've heard of economic self-interest, but not *thymos*.'

'No, they prefer not to clutter our children's brains with such concepts when they teach consumer logic and transcendental trading. But *thymos* is little more than the child in the playground who says, "Look at me; I can do this." There is no doubt that this instinct does last into adulthood, and is often powerful in human motivation. However, the child soon learns that impressing his or her peers is hard work and, even when successful, the results are short-lived. The other children have to be impressed with something else, and then something else if their admiration is to be maintained. *Thymos* could become something of a treadmill. Human beings are motivated by many things not associated with *thymos*. First there are individual pleasures and passions: solitude, company, friendship, rest, thought, eating good food, eating any food, making things, solving problems, compassion, pointless cruelty, irrational love and irrational hatred, to name but a few and not even the most obvious.'

'Not friendship surely; that must be influenced by a desire for recognition.'

'No, I think not. Most people who are successfully motivated by *thymos* have a group of friends with whom they can relax and be themselves – friends who will perhaps tease them. A person whose every relationship was *thymotic* would, I believe, be a very unstable and unhappy person.'

'The second category of motivations? The ones that aren't pleasures.'

'Ah yes, this is where it becomes more controversial, mainly because, in my opinion, these motivations have all but disappeared from our society. They are the social motivations of loyalty, sacrifice, duty, justice and solidarity. They are much ridiculed now as they were in the final years of the history period. Loyalty is perhaps the most important example because it applies not just to people, but also to religions, beliefs and ideas. I am going to give you just one example from history, which was discussed in a samizdat paper I recently received from the EU. One of the EU states called Italy was once divided up into different kingdoms and principalities, some of which were under foreign domination. They were united mainly through the efforts of a man called Garibaldi who landed in one part of the country with a thousand men and defeated two kingdoms and a well-equipped army of seventy thousand men. Apparently the country is covered with pompous equestrian statues of Garibaldi meeting the liberal king in whose name he was carrying out Italian unification. They shake hands on horseback like two equals. The real story is much more interesting. The king had been preceded by his cooks and other servants to the nearest town, where he was to banquet and enjoy the victory that was not his. The victor, on the other hand, left with a handful of loyal supporters for the nearest farmyard they could find, and ate bread, cheese and water. The water was tainted and Garibaldi became ill. We are all contradictory, but Garibaldi was more contradictory than most: he was an internationalist who fought a nationalist revolution, a republican who fought for a king, and pacifist who seemed happier and younger in the midst of battle. Off the battlefield, he was a solitary man who refused all honours and all the trappings of power. He was consumed by a political objective, not a desire to be celebrated. He was therefore not motivated by *thymos*, but by loyalty to ideas, certainly, and probably other more complex factors we may never understand fully – enjoyment of danger and hardship may well have been among them. He was briefly the dictator of two kingdoms and had their treasuries at his disposal, but after relinquishing power he left for his secluded home on the Isle of Caprera with only a supply of coffee, a drink he found indispensable.'

'So why are there no Garibaldis now?'

'Adolphus, you have asked the fundamental question,' Linklater said approvingly. 'And I believe I can give you the answer... or at least one of the answers, one of the contributing factors. Garibaldi, a sea captain's son, was brought up with stories of Roman greatness, and he was particularly influenced by the stories of Republican Rome. One Roman hero was called Cincinnatus and when the Rome was in great danger he was elected Dictator. After he had defeated Rome's enemy and made the country safe, he refused all wealth and honours, and returned to his farm, just as Garibaldi did nearly two and half millennia later. The important thing is not whether the story of Cincinnatus was true, but that the story was taught as a moral example in the society in which Garibaldi lived. We are the stories we tell ourselves, although there is always an element of choice. Garibaldi might have been influenced by the story of Caesar and used his military talents in a very different way. But our stories provide us with a moral language.'

'So what is wrong with the stories we tell ourselves now? Are they about *thymos* and economic self-interest?'

Linklater laughed. 'Strangely enough,' he said, 'our stories are not on the whole about that, although they often imply the absolutely normality, indeed righteousness, of such drives. The problem is that *thymos* and self-interest would not create good stories or even bad ones. Stories have a logic of their own. Many of the films churned out in the late history period were obsessed with revenge – personal and private revenge. Some terrible crime is committed and the hero sets off on an individual quest of revenge. The revenge is often horrendously cruel, but the hero emerges entirely uncorrupted and in some way cleansed by the experience, which is about as probable as Atlas holding up the heavens as punishment for the Titans' rebellion against the gods. This obsession with revenge is odd because over the previous millennium, storytelling had been teaching people first that revenge belonged to God and later that it belonged to the state. The cult of individual violence was one of the most disturbing phenomena of the late twentieth century.'

'So we need our stories of heroes back?'

'You ask a lot of me, Adolphus. I am not here to give you the answers – I am here to give you the questions. For heroes to be useful as moral exemplars they must, generally speaking, be dead. The trouble with the twentieth century was that all the heroes were alive and in power: Lenin, Hitler, Stalin, Mussolini, Mao Tse Tung and endless other dictators of left and right, each preaching his own absolute truth. What Fukuyama overlooks is that if recognition can be gained from others, then others must be willing to give it and indeed predisposed to give it – something that also disproves his theory that everyone is either in search of it or in pursuit of their own self-interest. Living heroes are so dangerous, because they can abuse the power that derives from their status, and few are willing, like Garibaldi, to reject that power when it is laid at their feet. However, I suspect that few people in Italy today respect the historical figure of Garibaldi any more than they respect the legendary one of Cincinnatus.'

'So loyalty is good or bad? I don't understand.'

'Loyalty to anything can be good, and even when mistaken it

has a tragic quality, but absolute loyalty becomes fanaticism and that is wholly dangerous. There is a ghastly man called Foxtrotter, a so-called official dissident who mixes with the shadowy establishment of our supposedly "lean" state and writes tedious books on political philosophy that no one reads. They wheel him out every now and then to provide a little more variety than the "constructive opposition" provided by either the New Freedom Party or the New Liberty Party. But on one thing Foxtrotter and I are as one: there must be no repetition of the age of ideology, if by ideology we mean that absurd loyalty to symbols and leaders, rather than balanced and moderate attachment to well-debated ideas and genuinely achievable objectives.'

'I've met him,' I interrupted.

'Who?'

'Michael Foxtrotter. I was sent to see him by Captain Younce.'

Linklater looked slightly put out, and momentarily lost his way. 'I must say, Adolphus, you've been attracting a lot of attention recently. What did you think of him?'

'Well, I didn't really understand a lot of what he was saying. I didn't like him, to be honest. I can't put my finger on the reason. Perhaps it was just because he seemed to talk down to me.'

'That is as maybe,' said Linklater, visibly reassured. 'He has a point though: ideology can be dangerous, as can fanatical religion. If I have a grand ambition, it is this: I would like to see history start again. I doubt I will see it in my lifetime, but it would be better if it came earlier rather than later. I fear that the later it comes, the more tempestuous and brutal the change will be. We have long ago spent yesterday's money gifted to society by yesterday's hard work, and we are fast using up what's left of tomorrow's by borrowing from the future to spend today. But most importantly we are building up a moral debt with the Third World which our future generations will have to pay. How will this other world treat us when it finally breaks through the technological barrier that defends us? Will they take their revenge? It would be only human if they did. If only we could act now with magnanimity – we could avoid a holocaust. If the army of the ragged swept through our malls and gated communities, would it hold itself back or would it unleash the most terrible reckoning? History teaches us to expect the worse. Although all violence is, in my opinion, inherently wrong, I do distinguish between the contemptible and thoughtless violence of the powerful with their smug prejudices, and the violence of the powerless who shake off the evil of the powerful and prove incapable of temperance. The trouble is that violence, if successful, simply turns the powerless into caricatures of the powerful. The blindness of those who have newly acquired power is often darker and more erratic than the darkness of those who have just lost power.'

'Is there no way we can avoid this tragedy?'

'I fear that we are too mean-spirited and our children too pampered to keep the dam from breaking in the most pitiable and dramatic manner.'

'And who gives you the right to start history again, if it could be such a traumatic event?'

'Certainly, we have to avoid the megalomania of our own ideas, but let me explain: history has never really ended, nor can it. Even the official End-Of-History Policy has had its own history. It started as a vague idea to celebrate the achievements and permanence of the "liberal democratic state", which were publicised through the Fukuyama End-Of-History Theme Parks. Capitalism had brought about a rollercoaster of change in every sphere of human life – work, love, family, war, religion, the arts – but by the late twentieth century that change became increasingly superficial. Given the continuous drive to bring costs down and guarantee risk-free investment, investors posed the question of whether there was any real point in continuously bringing out innovations when every innovation looked so much like the last one. Wouldn't it be better to simply recycle the great mass of existing material, whether it be in the field of architecture, clothing, music or anything else? In the early twenty-first century, the obsession with the present in terms of share prices, fashion, ideas and generally the "next-best-thing" had become such that the present seemed to destroy both the future and the past, indeed the future and the past became almost subversive. For a bit, the past survived solely in order to celebrate the present and demonstrate how lucky we are, but after a while, even that became questionable – hence the demise of the Fukuyama End-Of-History Theme Parks.'

'You might call it the politicisation of time?'

'Exactly,' he continued. 'Mankind has always been obsessed with time. In the past, it has been the cause of his megalomania: the terrible and destructive drive for immortality, which manifests itself in Herculean but ultimately vain attempts to leave something for posterity. But it was also the source of creativity, as people were only too aware of the brevity of their lives. Before the idea of progress, people looked to the past for a golden age, not to the future and certainly not to the present. In a sense, the End-Of-History marked the defeat of the idea of progress, which itself had defeated the idea of an ideal past. The future triumphed over the past, and then the present triumphed over the future. Everything has been reduced to the present, which constantly repeats itself or appears to repeat itself.'

'Isn't it a rather absurd propaganda campaign that no one can really believe in?'

'Now you're really thinking like an uncarded person,' he said with subdued delight. 'I used to think that this extreme attempt at doing away with different years was an absurd excess of bureaucratic zeal, but I now realise there was an intelligent mind behind it. Even for those of us who are very sensitive to the different trends affecting our society, it is very difficult to keep an accurate track of time. Every year, the same news is published on the same date: the same bomb outrage, the same society wedding, the same capture of Osama bin Laden's number two. Of course, some minor items are still changeable, and they still have to fine-tune an extremely complex system, but generally the newspaper for, say, 4 July of one year is the same as the one for the year before. The result is that historically we are completely disoriented. Osama bin Laden is one of the few people they have kept going from the "historical period". Obviously he has been dead for many years, but according to our media he is still plotting to destroy our cherished freedoms and way of life. And that way of life will eventually become a complete sense of timelessness, in which all the emphasis will be on rationalised consumption, while an unending war against terrorism justifies the temporary removal of all democratic rights. When I say I would like history to start again, I mean that I would like a return to democracy and a return to debate based on reliable information, which is now entirely lacking.'

'So if human history has not really ended and there is no predictable end other than extinction of the species, when did history start if we evolved over time?'

'This is a fascinating question, one of those fascinating questions that everyone should answer in their own fashion without getting too excited about it, because no sooner do you settle on one position than somebody throws in some more information that turns everything upside down. I enjoy working through books on this subject from the history period, and I can only tell you what my latest interpretation is. But it will no doubt change, if I am left in peace. A man called Rousseau argued that the first man to fence off a piece of land and call it his own destroyed equality and created slavery. I thought this was nonsense – a romanticisation or at least a gross simplification of events too distant to pronounce upon. That was until I read this.' Linklater then pulled out a work he clearly loved and placed it on the table. For a few moments he leafed quickly through the book, and his familiarity soon found the page he sought. 'Ah, here we are!' he cried. 'This much more recent writer, a historian, examines life in what were called hunter gatherer societies – before agriculture was invented. Listen: "The big question about the hunter-gatherers, therefore, does not seem to be *How did they progress towards the higher level of an agricultural and politicised society? But What persuaded them to abandon the secure, well-provided and psychologically liberating advantages of their primordial life-style?*" In the myth of Eden, I realised, it was not sex or nakedness that was revealed to Adam and Eve by eating the apple, it was agriculture, and consequently property and all-consuming work that leaves little room for anything else. And unequal labour as Rousseau had already guessed. It meant large families rather than small families, because children were a source of manpower. It meant endless expansion and the subjugation of nature.

'Marxists argued that "Property is theft". This is nonsensical because theft presupposes the concept of property – the social attribution of *stuff* to particular individuals or groups of individuals. It should be "There would be no theft without property". But property invented many other evils: power, greed, covetousness, slavery and brutally stupefying labour – and also many goods: creative labour, generosity, magnanimity and solidarity beyond one's own group. Property marked the end of the age of innocence and widened the gap between good and evil. It created our civilisations and all the comforts and pleasures we enjoy: our buildings, our machines, our medicines and the diversification of our skills. It also created war, expropriation, and ever greater extremes of power. It did not make us more skilled and intelligent and it did not create song, art and poetry, which must have predated agriculture, but it did create the accumulation of song, art and poetry, so that each generation could build on the previous one. It made us who we are: civilised man, with all that is good and bad in that. There is no way back. Innocence, once lost, can never be regained.

'If I have a utopia, a very vague utopia, then it is a society of individual freedom in which property is not abolished but subjugated to the needs of society as a whole – a society which values not wealth but creativity and skill. It's alright to invent utopias as long as you do not want to enforce them immediately by any means. Political action must always start from where you are now and not where you would ideally like to be.'

'So what can we do in the place where we are now?'

'Very little, I'm afraid,' he stared at me grimly. 'All we can do at the moment is collect information, reliable information, and spread it around amongst those who still care. It is called a samizdat system. I am at the centre of it, which is why Younce is so interested in me. We are little more than a reading club, and we rely a great deal on material that arrives from the European Union. As democratic rights are gradually eroded over there as well, it's becoming increasingly difficult to function. The quality of our information is deteriorating, particularly as far as events in the Third World are concerned. I have a list of about two hundred recipients: they are people from all walks of life, whose activity consists solely in receiving material, reading it and possibly handing it on – a risk that is entirely their own. When Younce picks me up – and I sense that this is imminent – these people will be cut off from the samizdat network unless I can find someone else to take on my work. After careful consideration, I have decided that you are that person – the right person.'

'Why me?'

'I may not be the greatest conspirator; I am a man of ideas and a man of ideas is naturally garrulous. I am also a man who believes in humanity, so it is difficult for me to be in a situation where I have to distrust almost everyone I meet. I do, however, consider myself a reasonably good judge of character. When I met you, I knew instantly that you are naive – politically very naive, as is your entire generation – but I also sensed that you are someone of genuinely good instincts and a methodical brain. Once uncarded, I believe you to be as reliable a choice as any of the people involved in the movement, and I have to say that all the people I know in the movement are either dangerous hotheads or police spies.'

'What about Edith? Wouldn't she be a suitable choice?'

'Edith?' he repeated the question slowly and then continued in the same tone of hesitant deliberation. 'Edith is someone I greatly admire, but I have to say that I consider her to fall into the former category – that of dangerous hotheads. She has actually shown a great deal of interest in the samizdat project, but I have always kept her at arm's length as far as it is concerned. She has energy and undoubted talents, but she is not suited to this most important task. We're attempting to co-ordinate forms of non-violent protest in the Fukuyamas, and I think she could prove useful in this less intellectual activity. I hasten to add that it is not her intellect that I question; it is her lack of prudence. You, of course, have another enormous advantage: you have a BB and can move around a great deal more easily. Under the cover of pursuing illicit tastes for banned sexual relationships or banned cultural activities only permitted to BBs, you could go almost anywhere.'

This, of course, left me in a state of considerable confusion, which I tried to cover up as best I could. I was now in deep with Younce, Edith and Linklater. I had decided to betray Younce, or the decision had somehow been taken for me. I now faced another decision: was I to follow Edith and betray Linklater, or the other way around? The former considered the latter to be a police spy and the latter considered the former to be a dangerous hothead. It was enough to make your head spin, and there was no way of knowing who was right. I decided not to tell either about the confidences I had received from the other.

Linklater took me on a confusing tube journey, which involved changing at an unnecessary amount of stations. Finally in one particular station, he indicated the position of a loose tile without using his hands, and explained that behind the tile I could find a computer disk that contained the mailing list for his part of the samizdat project. After several more apparently pointless changes from one train to another, we divided and left for our separate homes.

CHAPTER THIRTEEN

The Act of Sabotage

NERO HAS ONE of those faces that can't stop grinning. And the permanent grin reveals a set of jagged uneven teeth. Strangely the grin narrowly avoids appearing vacuous and comes across as a symptom of irrepressible contentment. He has a large straight pointed nose and tiny brown eyes set deep in his skull. The top of his head is bald, and he disguises it by cutting the rest of his hair down to a very short black and grey stubble. This gives full prominence to a set of extremely large and misshapen ears. In spite of the unfortunate shape of most of the constituent elements of his physiognomy, the whole manages to come across as engaging and friendly, probably because of that permanent grin and his undoubted self-confidence.

The first time I saw that now detestable face it was framed by the open window of his gleaming new car. Edith was in the passenger seat, her smile betraying a disturbing edginess. The instant I sat down on the back seat, the car powered away and flung me backwards, making it difficult to complete the action of closing the car door.

'We're getting a bomb,' said Edith excitedly.

'Now? Today? I thought it was tomorrow.' I felt sick. In spite of having been instructed by Younce to play along with their plan, the unexpected immediacy of its implementation terrified me. 'Now? I don't think Linklater is too keen on violent action.'

'Fuck Linklater,' guffawed Nero, 'he's just a comfortable, middle-class revolutionary who doesn't really give a damn about anything. What does he know about guerrilla warfare?'

'It *is* a non-violent action,' said Edith more seriously; 'we're only going to hit them economically by blowing up a railway in the middle of the night. Nero's right: if we go at Linklater's pace, this regime will have destroyed the world before we get round to doing anything. The situation demands urgent action.' This argument entirely disregarded her previous claim that Linklater was a police spy. It appeared that his perception of her was more well-founded.

'I don't think I'm in,' I said in a slow and tremulous voice.

'Fuck it, Adolphus!' Edith cried, 'are you a man or a mouse? We've discussed this often enough – I thought you were in agreement.'

'Well, not really. But anyway I thought it was more hypothetical.'

The car screeched to halt and Nero turned round in his seat. His grin had disappeared, perhaps the only occasion this ever happened so completely. Without the grin, his is a terrifying face, the kind of face that can deprive you of all rational thought. An animal face that reduces you to another animal – a scared and bewildered one. Instinct triggers instinct. 'Are you in or are you out? Because if you're out, you'll find yourself in that ditch over there with your throat slit so wide that they'll be able to see what you had for breakfast if they look one way and your excuse for a brain if they look the other.' He pressed the point home by drawing his right index finger across his neck.

'Hold on, Nero!' said Edith in a shocked voice. 'There was no need for that. We are all volunteers: if Adolphus wants to go, that's up to him.'

She had put her hand on Nero's shoulder in a gesture of remonstration, but he just shrugged her off and went for me again. 'Listen, creep! Are you in or not? This is not some Sunday-school outing.'

'I'm in,' I capitulated in a feeble almost inaudible voice and at the same time I flushed with terror.

'Good! Well, that's okay then,' he proclaimed triumphantly, and his grin returned instantaneously. 'Let's get on with it.'

The rest of the journey was subdued. I could feel Edith's discomfort. He, on the other hand, just gave the impression of a man who likes driving rather fast to the office. He drew up the car at a nightclub with the unnecessary screeching of brakes so typical of his style. The illuminated sign declared, 'The Popping Poppies, Pop Music That Gets Everyone Jumping', and above the writing two anthropomorphised and rather androgynous poppies were dancing the twist.

'Not exactly my scene,' grinned the irrepressible Nero, 'but still work is work.' That was the second statement of the night that alarmed me: it did not seem typical of a revolutionary, even a fanatical and apparently bloodthirsty one, as he was clearly supposed to be; nor did it seem typical of a carded citizen, who is not generally known for his work ethic. I was aware of being dragged into something dark and ugly, but I had no idea of how to get out without exciting Nero's homicidal tendencies.

We ordered drinks and waited for our contact at the bar. At that moment Constantia appeared: 'Adolphus, fancy seeing you here! I heard you got a BB.' She smiled emptily but also a little sadly. That sadness touched me, and touches me now. She too is part of the reason I am doing what I am doing now.

Constantia had many attributes and was in many ways an

attractive woman: of average height with a slender body, regular features and black black hair, but she failed to be really attractive because her eyes, although large and dark, were filled with a timid bewilderment, a fear of life that triggered senseless giggling or senseless chatter. It wasn't so much stupidity that made her do this as a desperate need to fit in, coupled with an absolute certainty that she would never be able to do so. We lived together for a year, and even went as far as registering our relationship for tax purposes. Once the passionless affair came to its gradual and inevitable end, I felt a kind of brotherly companionship towards her.

'Gosh, fancy knowing a real BB,' she effused. 'I bet you get up to some really exciting things now, Adolphus. Of course, you won't want to stick around the likes of me any more. Now you've got new friends,' and she nodded shyly towards Edith.

'Piss off,' said Edith curtly, 'we've got things to do.'

'Sorry, I didn't mean to intrude,' replied Constantia through a puckered expression. She then turned around and rushed off. That was the last time I saw her: her slim back darting away - innocence that was swallowed up in the dark density of the crowd.

'That was unnecessary,' I reproached Edith.

'We're not here to chat up old girlfriends,' she retorted, and Nero grinned.

A man in a grey suit appeared. He was holding a black sports bag, and looked very out of place. He recognised Nero immediately and made straight for us without talking. He placed the bag next to Nero, while asking the barman for directions to a local cinema. He then left. A relaxed and businesslike Nero told us that he would take the bag, while we were to circulate and then come out to the car after exactly five minutes. He would prime the device so that we could leave immediately for the selected spot on the railway line.

We waited in silence for the interminable five minutes. As we came out of the nightclub, we could see Nero in his car on the other side of the car park. He waved to us to hurry up, and for a few yards we even quickened our step. Then suddenly Edith stopped: 'Something's not right. I saw him leaving... Christ, he never took the bag!' She turned on her heels and started to run towards the nightclub. When she was fifteen yards away, the door and windows of the nightclub illuminated with an orange-yellow light and again I heard the dull and deathly thud that carries with it a blast of hot sickly air. Edith was on the ground with several cuts from flying glass. The only serious one was a gash across her left cheek, the only sign she was aware of it was the instinctive movement of her left hand to wipe the blood away. 'The bastards, the bastards, they never told me about this. They killed all those people,' she added incredulously, 'they killed all those people. Why?' By now she was standing up and wanted to run towards what remained of the nightclub. Two people had been blown right out of the club and lay groaning on the tarmac. She seemed to want to help them, but I restrained her. I remembered the last bomb and how quickly the police arrived.

'Edith, there's nothing you can do,' I shouted, 'we must get going. We must get out of here.' We turned and ran. As we did so, Nero circled round to us in the car and ordered us to jump in.

When Edith saw him, she started to shout, 'Fuck off, you murdering bastard. The bomb was already set when that man brought it, and you knew – you knew all along. Why, why?' She raised her fists to hit the car, but the car and Nero were already gone. She grabbed my hand, and pulled me with her across the car park to some gardens. We then made our way from one garden to another for about half a mile. 'All the roads will have been sealed off long ago,' she explained, 'we must move quietly but quickly if we are to get out of here.'

CHAPTER FOURTEEN

The Scolding

WE MADE IT to my house. We couldn't think of anywhere else to go, and besides, our society which no longer has many travellers over long distances is short on hotels and guest houses. We sat on my sofa in a stunned and unbroken silence, and for a long time we held each other – no so much out of affection, more as one drowning person might cling to another in the belief that they have grabbed onto something that floats. I don't know what her thoughts were, but mine revolved around my different reactions to the bomb in Thatcher Square and this more recent one at the Popping Poppies Nightclub. In the first case, I had experienced it as a terrible incident, but one I was detached from. I never gave it a great deal of thought. I knew no one who was involved, and I had no idea what caused it, much as you might view some terrible natural calamity: horrific, unavoidable and the chances of personal involvement are lower than a road accident. The papers said it was probably Al-Qaeda. People who hate us were responsible, but fortunately we have our hard-working police and intelligence services to protect us. In the case of the second bomb, I knew everything. I knew that the bomb was placed by Nero in order to cause the maximum number of casualties. I knew that Edith and I were partially implicated. I was acting on Captain Younce's instructions, and at the time I doubted he could have known the intended target. Edith was completely exposed and I had to protect her. I also knew enough about this intelligence work to know that I could not definitely rely on Younce's protection, and yet there could be no doubt that men like him were needed if psychopaths like Nero were loose in society. The thing I really couldn't get out of my mind was the sight of Constantia walking away after Edith had insulted her. If someone like her – someone who demands so little of life – is at risk, then there really is no justice in this world. I know that is absurd. Of course, there is no justice – although I once thought there was. No, it is that some events describe a reality so perfectly. This girl, my companion, with whom I had lain at night, had been murdered along with many others by some fanatic of uncertain ideals, and I was implicated. The last time she saw me, I was standing next to her murderer. I felt I was her murderer, and the thing was tearing me apart. I shrugged off Edith's embrace with some force and jumped to my feet. I was prey to two powerful emotions: one was the chasm of guilt I have just described and the other was anger at all these people who had pushed their way into my perfect life and destroyed everything, including my ex-girlfriend, with whom perhaps I could have reconnected. Younce, Linklater, Foxtrotter, Edith and, most sinister of all, Nero – what had I to do with them? They came from another planet.

We looked at each other with hostile stares. She probably read the accusation in my eyes, and I certainly read the defiance in hers. Possibly we were about to start an argument, but the doorbell rang. An ashen-faced Linklater rushed into the room. 'What the hell's going on? What have you been up to?'

We were stunned that he knew anything at all. By way of an answer to our unspoken questions, he went straight to the television, switched on the 24-hour news and then waited. Eventually the newsreader announced yet another bomb outrage, this time in a nightclub. The forces of public order were however hard on the heels of the perpetrators. Then they showed a CCTV picture of Nero, Edith and me entering the club. The quality of the images was very poor and you would really have had to have known us first, if you were to recognise us from the pictures. In the case of Nero, recognition was entirely out of the question.

Linklater turned around sternly: 'Adolphus, I had more faith in you.'

It was Edith who took my part: 'He didn't want to take part – and anyway it was meant to be a soft economic target with no casualties.'

'So what happened? Did you guys leave and forget to take the bomb with you,' Linklater sarcastically emphasised each syllable.

'I know, I know,' said Edith, now sitting on the sofa again and holding her head in her hands. 'He must have planned it right from the beginning.'

'Who planned it? Do you mean Adolphus?'

'No, of course not,' she cried, 'Nero. It was Nero.'

'Nero! You haven't been mixing with that delinquent? I always had him down as a police spy.'

I was now hunched in the armchair. 'When you people dislike someone, you always accuse him of being a police spy!' I broke into the conversation.

'You're right; we cannot be sure that he is a spy,' admitted Linklater grimly. 'Adolphus, why didn't you mention this action when we spoke?'

'Edith said that you too are a police spy. I didn't know who to believe,' I protested rather pathetically.

Linklater laughed: 'Edith, I knew you were wild, but I never took you for stupid.'

She smiled blankly and merely uttered, 'Well, we all make mistakes.'

'I have told you both again and again,' said Linklater, 'that we must only engage in non-violent action. The reasons are clear. Firstly, violence is morally wrong and that is an absolute. Secondly, we don't know who is responsible for this violence, but one thing is clear: any form of terrorist violence simply strengthens the government and puts off the day when we, as a society, can have a proper debate about the very real economic and ecological problems that are building up all the time, not to speak of the impossible misery of the Third World. Thirdly and perhaps most importantly, violence irreparably corrupts the perpetrator of violence, however justified the cause. Violence turns the dissident into a mirror image of the thing he is criticising. That in part is why it plays into the hands of the establishment, because it forms a smokescreen to obscure the real issues. But also,' and here he looked at us with both compassion and a certain schoolmasterly severity, 'look what it does to you! Violence is the product of either hate or contempt. Hate destroys the hater; it eats away at his soul. Contempt? Well, contempt is for them; it cannot be an acceptable emotion for anyone who is genuinely concerned with the fate of humanity.'

Edith and I were bent beneath the weight of our shame – and a strange sense of unreality.

'It's all very well to talk of non-violence,' said Edith without raising her head and in a voice tremulous with intense emotion, 'if you are a wealthy lawyer, but what about those whose pitiful conditions cannot wait for a possible period of enlightenment in a distant future? We Fukuyama people are an oppressed people in limbo, and citizens don't give a shit. And they only will if it affects their lives, and that involves some form of violence, even if it is only directed at economic targets.'

'Edith, you have no idea which of us two will make old bones. Anyone who challenges this regime puts their life on the line, whatever their social position – even if they are a BB,' he added pointing at me. 'Fortunately for me and my temperament, we will live in a time when non-violent protest is not only right, it is absolutely the only practical form of action we can engage in. There are periods in history, such as during the Second World War, when limiting oneself to non-violent action may have been wrong. But I am talking of a very extreme situation in which people were being annihilated by the million for belonging to a particular race or holding particular views. But even the most justifiable violent action necessarily corrupts those who carry it out. The beauty of non-violent action is that it is not just a means to an end, it is an end in itself. It concerns the whole way you relate to other people. It means turning the other cheek. It means caring nothing about your own death. It means knowing that there is no justice, but hoping that by spreading a culture of non-violence that justice will finally appear. And yes, that will be in some distant future.'

'While people rot. People were not only annihilated in your war, they were annihilated in my short lifetime. Where are the Abkhazians, where are the Chechnyans?' Edith raised her head defiantly.

'I am just as horrified by those things as you. I wish I could be an optimist, but I lack the powers of self-deception. You have to understand that non-violence is a liberation in itself, and it is the only liberation we will ever experience.

'I don't rate your chances of avoiding the intelligence services for long,' Linklater added bluntly. 'Your best chance would be to make for Brighton, where there are still a few places to stay, and they're more used to people drifting in and out. Adolphus, don't use your BB identity card. It will only attract attention,

and remember national security always takes precedence over
BB privileges. Here's some money, and I suggest you don't touch
your bank accounts for several months. They've probably been
frozen, anyway. You'd have a better chance without her, as she
doesn't have proper papers and is a Fukuyama fugitive. But I
sense there is something between you… Adolphus, I'll change
the hiding-place for that material I told you about, because if
they get you – and they almost certainly will – they will get it
out of you.'

Linklater did not wish us luck or give us any goodbyes. He
rushed out as quickly as he came in. Edith, always surprisingly
well-equipped for a Fukuyama girl, produced a mobile phone
and started to send a text message. I added my sense of having
let Linklater down to my sense of having betrayed Constantia.
The world that then surrounded me bore no relation to the world
I thought I knew when I first met Younce at the top of the
escalator.

CHAPTER FIFTEEN

On The Run

THE CHANGEABLE WEATHER of Brighton in the spring reflected our uncertain moods. We found a guest house on the seafront. At first, we kept each other at arm's length. There was no reason why we shouldn't have split up. I didn't trust Edith, and her attitude to me was inconsistent. Sometimes it appeared contemptuous, at others almost protective. As Linklater had suggested, I had most to lose from our continued liaison. On my own, I could have probably made it to the continent and from there to some reasonably comfortable country just beyond the borders of the European Union. Sexual attraction undoubtedly played its part in my loyalty to her, although in the early days on the run I was not aware of it. I held her responsible for my situation, but also cherished an irrational belief in our common fate.

She was undoubtedly miserable. Her attempt to retrieve the bag from the nightclub proved that she was not knowingly party to the atrocity. Her silences were impenetrable. Late-winter rain trapped us for much of the time in our room. On the fourth day, the sun greeted us in the breakfast room, and sliced across our table. One side was so bright, you had to screw up your eyes; the other was a reminder of our miserable past. When put in contrast, all dualities dazzle us: understanding and misunderstanding, knowledge and ignorance, loyalty and disloyalty, happiness and unhappiness. Although we can separate them easily enough as concepts, we find them more difficult to separate as things we experience. During this period on the run, such dazzling contrasts heightened my senses but also confused them; both the awareness and the confusion provided me with a kind of anxious happiness. Contrary to the tenets of the ruling ideology, happiness is not a right but a random and often unconscious gift. Edith sat on the sunny side of the table in a halo of dust particles, her features enlivened by light and shade – a picture of youth, energy and the ability to take fortune by the scraggy neck and bend it to one's own will. In that moment her self-confidence was a conscious decision to overcome the dark events from which we had fled. She insisted on chatting to me brightly, while I continued to rebuff her. At the end of the meal, she put her hand on mine: 'I know you hate me. Perhaps you are right to do so.' I now understand that she had convinced herself she could resolve our problems.

Always predictable in my reactions, I simply melted and muttered that I didn't hate her at all. 'Not at all,' I added more assertively.

'Come back up to the room with me,' she said, and on the first day in which we could have finally left our room, we returned to it to make love. And she really did make love this time. The difference between it and our previous more perfunctory encounters meant they were like two entirely different experiences. The reason for this change in her was still unclear. Was it our shared proximity to death and the danger of imminent arrest? Was it her fear of being left alone? Was it her love for me, as she would protest so loudly in a more recent encounter? Or was it something else?

It will seem strange, even irresponsible, that after the terrible event at the nightclub, Edith and I found a kind of peace. The days slipped by quite easily. I have never been so close to anyone, or rather, I have never felt so close to anyone, because I now realise there was a great deal of distance between us.

Edith became very solicitous. She must have used some of Linklater's money to buy me some new clothes and smarten me up. Of course, the clothes I had were expensive, but in Edith's opinion they were not in good taste. My parents, who died in a car crash when I was in my teens, had been too busy pursuing the imperative to consume to take a great deal of interest in their only child. I was not, therefore, used this kind of attention, and I enjoyed it. I was flattered by it. Occasionally Edith would dust a crumb from the shoulder of my jacket or adjust my collar, and this could be followed by a light kiss to my cheek or my forehead if I was seated. She was physical, but her physicality was as maternal as it was sexual. Edith was concerned. Edith was concerned about me.

One morning we were sitting outside a café on the seafront. Brighton, like all our cities and town, does not have a large population but it does have more than the average. A trickle of intrepid holidaymakers and day-trippers still makes its way down to the beach – a cultural remnant from the days of cheap oil and cheap travel. On the whole they looked reasonably affluent. In a society with a vast chasm between those on citizens' benefit and the ultra rich, this middle class is probably the smallest of the three classes. That day, they seemed to be a purposeful, perhaps well-balanced group as they played with their children, built sandcastles and did the things that visitors to the seaside should do. I remembered that Linklater had once told me that it appeared from his historical studies that no class was inherently good or bad: like nations and generations, they contained good and bad. It could be said that when a class begins to assert itself it is creative and bold, and when it is in decay it is wonderfully introspective, nostalgic and liberated by its powerlessness, but when it is well-established and at the height of its powers, it is smug and conservative in the worst sense of the word. In this, it is no different to any other intelligent being, whether individual or social. Linklater also told me that in the late history and early End-of-History periods, the middle class was enormous and very powerful. But during the End-of-History period, the middle class had withered and the only profession to flourish was the legal one. The new Consuming Class, which has taken its place, is mainly made up of rentiers but also includes those on Citizens' Benefit. These holidaymakers were spending their day in activities that involved little exchange of money and went undetected by the statistics on GDP. Edith found them extremely irritating, even pathetic. She sat behind her sunglasses and passed comment on them as they went past, dragging their children and engaging in conversation. 'Don't they have anything better to do?'

'Well I, for one, would be very happy to change places with them,' I muttered. 'Better to be a family man on a reasonable income than a fabulously wealthy BB on the run from the forces of law and order.'

'Of course, darling,' she said putting her hand on mine. 'Who knows? Perhaps one day we will have a family.'

Today this conversation seems a cruel joke, but at the time I was genuinely moved. 'That is what I dream of,' I allowed myself to be carried away.

'Then Adolphus, you must put your trust in me.' She fidgeted, not quite sure how to move on to the most delicate part of our conversation. 'Adolphus, you know how Linklater said he was going to move something just before he left your house.'

'Yes.'

'What was he going to move?'

'I'm afraid I can't tell you that, Edith,' I said firmly.

'Adolphus, this is not like you to be so stubborn. You have to tell me, because it is very important for our future together. You have to trust me.'

'Edith, I would like to tell you, believe me, but I have already betrayed Linklater's trust once, and I can't possibly do it again.'

'So Linklater is more important to you than I am,' she rasped with syllabic clarity – with terrible predictability.

I sighed. I wanted to tell her. I wanted to tell her everything, including the location of the computer disk, but something told me that amongst all the grand ideas and personal sacrifices it would be mean-spirited to give away a secret simply because you liked the way someone brushed a crumb from the shoulder of your jacket. Was I so small that I would let myself be swayed by the smallest of things, while every person on that list had put their lives at risk because they wanted a better world? 'I'm sorry, Edith,' I said, now rather enjoying my principled stand and sounding slightly pompous, 'I simply cannot betray the trust Linklater placed in me – not even to you, my darling, who I trust even more than life itself.'

Edith seemed singularly unimpressed by the 'darling', the trust-more-than-life stuff or the grandeur of my moral high ground. 'Listen, jerk,' she hissed as she stood up to go, 'it's going to cost you more than life itself, if you don't watch it. How can you be so stupid?' In standing up so quickly, she knocked the tray out of the waitress's hands. The coffee cups crashed to the pavement with an unpleasant and discordant clatter. Heads at the few occupied tables turned with half-interested and half-excited expressions, hoping, willing some more action to fill the empty day. They got it. Edith reacted to the waitress's complaint by telling her to fuck off and pushing her hard with her strong sinewy arms. The waitress landed on the ground, but even then

Edith didn't let up. 'So big fucking deal! You've lost a couple of coffee cups. Some people lose their families, some people lose their countries, some people lose their livelihoods, and they don't whinge about it, you stupid bitch.' At this point Edith took out a note from the money Linklater had given us and threw it down on the prostrate waitress, who muttered something about calling the police.

'Do me a favour,' cried Edith, 'call the police. You have no idea what a favour that would be. It might just get me out of this mess. Call the police, but I don't think they'll come running for two coffee cups.' She started to move away, but then returned to push back to the ground the unfortunate waitress who had pulled herself half-way up. 'Two fucking coffee cups. You want another ten dollars. Here, take them. Two fucking coffee cups. People are not allowed to express themselves. People are not allowed to create. People are locked up in crazy detention centres because they or their parents were born in the wrong part of the globe. People leave bombs all over the place. People die. People are going to die, and nobody really knows why. And you, little Miss I'm so hard done by because I work for two hours at a café on the seafront, are upset about two coffee cups. Here, take another ten dollars. That's all you care about.'

No one at the other tables moved, but I heard a 'Disgraceful behaviour!' in a man's voice. That was when Edith left with a brisk stride, and I immediately began to run after her. I don't know where I acquired this desperate need to placate, so different from Edith's powerful ability to confront. I caught up with her, and barely glancing sideways at me she said, 'What the fuck do you want?'

'I want you to understand.'

She stopped walking and turned towards me. 'I do understand, stupid. I do understand. You are the one who does not understand. I wish I could make you understand, but you are too innocent, too foolish.' She grabbed me by the neck in a way that was both affectionate and aggressive, as though she wanted to shake some sense into me. She did in fact gently shake my head. 'Listen to me, Adolphus, tell me what I want to know and I can get us out of this mess.'

There is no one so stubborn as a weak man who has dug his heels in. 'No, I can't betray Linklater. I know that is the right thing to do. You should understand that.'

'Why are you doing this? It won't make any difference in the long run.' She then burst into tears and hugged me. That was the moment in which I nearly gave in. I cannot say why I didn't. Was it a moral decision? Was it loyalty to Linklater? Was I converted to the cause? Was it just a stupid stubbornness born of the desire to prove that I was a man of principle, a man who believed in principles and was not going to be moved by female wiles? Who knows what went on in my uncarded brain?

In that moment I realised that she occupied an entirely different viewpoint to mine – that she really did have a greater understanding of our situation. I should have told her what I knew and let her take control of the situation, but instead I followed the thought no further. It was not stupidity, but a need to cling to my dreams, and in my dreams I was her protector and she not mine.

Our clandestine existence continued, and my self-delusion increased. Edith attempted in various ways to get me to talk, and I began to treat it as a game in which I retained a measure of power. I thought about the possibility of getting Edith across the Channel, and fantasised about a permanent relationship with her as my lover beyond the borders of our consumer paradise. Another kind of paradise in which we would rediscover the cleansing, invigorating and uplifting life of hard work, perhaps on a piece of land. For me, Edith was a greater prize than a BB. Who wants to hang out with the boring rich? There were – there are things I want to discover about being a human being, an uncarded human being. I regret those years spent in the pursuit of wealth to obtain a licence for immoral behaviour. The only benefit of those hours of careful study of the market was the pleasure of the study itself and the anticipation of the hoped-for rewards. The rewards themselves proved delusory.

But then again, my dreams of domestic bliss with Edith were equally futile and absurd. I believe that really good relationships are difficult to find in any age. Many practical things can get in the way, even when a couple are well-matched. Well-matched is not how I would describe the relationship between me and Edith, and as for the practical obstacles, they were too many to mention. But living with impractical dreams was another feature of uncarded existence. I believe that in the history period people used to muddle on for decades in such deluded states, suffering the consequences when reality caught up with them, but often surviving to invent other dreams. It was perhaps not such a bad life. It was perhaps better than the sedated existence of a carded brain.

There was another incident during our stay in Brighton that I would like to write about. It did not concern us directly, but like the encounter with the man in the three-cornered hat, it made me think about the kind of the world that existed beyond the confines of our enlightened societies inhabited by the Last Man. We went into a bar to have a break from our endless argument about the information I wouldn't give Edith. There was a young man in a wheelchair throwing darts at a dartboard and then wheeling himself up to it to retrieve them. On one of these manoeuvres, he lifted the darts from the board with the skill of someone who clearly did little else all day long and turned his wheelchair to face us. Finding us there, he launched into an immediate attack, 'Like looking at a cripple, do we? Never seen a man with no legs before?' His eyes burnt with unquenchable anger and bitterness. He was a robust man in spite of his disability, with a strong, not unpleasant face whose regular features were hardened by suffering. He perhaps saw a weakness in me or a willingness to listen, for he wheeled his way up to me and grabbed my right forearm in a steely grip. He tugged me down and spoke hoarsely, 'This is what a man looks like when he has had both his legs blown off above the knee.'

'Leave the guy alone,' shouted the barman, 'we don't want any more of your war stories – you'll frighten off the customers.'

'No way,' he shouted back, 'they love my stories, don't you?' He fixed me with his manic eyes. 'You'd love to hear how I lost these two pins, wouldn't you?'

'I just came in for a drink,' I replied pathetically.

'Bring the man a drink – and the woman too,' the man in the wheelchair ordered magnanimously. 'What are you having?'

We allowed ourselves to be seated with our drinks opposite the man, perhaps out of a desire to exchange our own tragedies for somebody else's.

'I was in 'Stan,' he announced. 'Operation Extending Democracy and Justice.

'Where's 'Stan?' Edith asked.

'Pakistan. That's what we call Pakistan. We went in there a year ago and we went in hard. Really hard because the place is close to India and they didn't want to upset India too much; so we went in, caused havoc and came out fast. Wow, did we cause havoc. We shelled the cities, we bulldozed the cities and then collected so many of their young men that their women will never know a dick that's less than forty years old. We put the men up against walls and tied their wrists with plastic, good and tight like they train us to – and then lorries came along to take them away. God knows where they went. Wasn't my job to know where they went. We destroyed their orchards, their roads, their hospitals. I was an officer. All the men are recruited in the Fukuyamas these days. Not many citizens now have the stomach for that work. They don't care what happens as long as they don't have to risk their necks. But those Fukuyama boys are the salt of the earth – bad bastards every one of them. You don't want to be on the wrong side of those boys, I can tell you. They just strip a country to its bone, you see. They just destroy everything in sight and leave the native to pick up the pieces. Those Mujuhadeen in 'Stan won't be giving us any more trouble for many a long year, I can tell you that. We did a good job. We did a damn good professional job, me and my Fukuyama boys of the 55th English Infantry.'

'I'm sure you did,' I said submissively.

'I'm sure you bloody didn't,' said Edith, 'unless doing a good job means massacring men, women and children for no good reason at all. Because your government took a dislike to them.'

I was alarmed by this outburst, because the man's presence consisted solely of menace, or at least up to that moment. He seemed surprised by Edith's words, saddened. He changed his tone, 'No one has ever challenged me before. No one. Many things happened there that shouldn't have. They trained us in Nevada and got us all fired up with how the Mujuhadeen were going to invade the Federation any day now. But I can tell you there was nothing in 'Stan. Those Mujuhadeen, if they ever existed, couldn't have invaded the Isle of Wight. It was a cakewalk; we just let off ordnance all the way to Islamabad and never took a casualty until a mine exploded under my Humvee during the withdrawal. It killed three of my Fukuyama boys and it took my legs off.' He now looked tired.

'I like you, lady,' he addressed Edith. 'You've got balls. You remind me of my Fukuyama boys. How come you landed up with this pansy here? You understand about survival; I can see that. That's the one thing I learnt in 'Stan: how to know someone who knows how to survive. You can read it in their eyes. They sent me, a citizen with an RCI card, to 'Stan. What's the point of that? You can hardly be a rational consumer in a fucking war, can you? There's no programme for that – not for that shit. People here have no idea. I just tell them one side of the story – not the guilt, the nightmares, the terrible terrible sights that cannot be forgotten. I don't tell them that, because they wouldn't understand. But armies don't think, soldiers don't think, they can't. They just do what they're told and live with the consequences; that means the memories. You've got balls, and you're right: we did kill innocent people, people who had no chance.

'Our colonel gave us a pep talk before we went into Islamabad. "We've already softened up the target and we have depersonalised it," he said. "We've taken out the hospital, where the doctors were giving false reports on the casualties. We've picked up all the young male gooks fleeing the city with their families. Now all we got to do is go in and get the bad guys. This is a Hiroshima, an Inchon, a Hue City, a Fallujah. That was in the history period. In the End-of-History, we do this every year or so, and we've become dead good at what we do. I know I can count on everyone of you to do your duty and I don't have to tell you what that is – go kick some butt and make End-of-History." We all cheered, but when we went in, I could see that they hadn't depersonalised it very well: there were dead women and children everywhere. No one counted them. And maybe they were the lucky ones: the place was a wreck and there were tens of thousands of wounded. It was meant to be a victory, a great victory.'

He flicked the ash off his cigarette with an effeminate flourish that sat oddly with his macho spring-triggered aggressiveness. The gesture suggested that he might have become something other than the wounded soldier he was condemned to be for the rest of his life. The blast that removed his legs ended his soldiering but also condemned his essence to be that of a soldier forever. His luckier colleagues would embark on other careers that would eventually diminish their soldiering to an exciting but relatively brief experience of their youth; they would develop new essences, possibly in contrast with war. He would never discover his other selves as he threw his wheelchair abruptly around the barroom and threw darts with unnecessary force against an insentient target. We finished our drinks and took our leave. The ex-soldier, who now looked strangely relaxed, shook Edith's hand warmly and drawled in his mid-Atlantic English, 'Look after yourself, y'hear. You've got balls, lady, *cojones*; you come back any time. I'm always here throwing them darts. Bring your pansy, if you must.'

Then came the day when I returned to my room and one look at Edith told me her state of hopeful edginess was over, her concern for me was over and her desire to please was over. In their place was something coldly determined. When I asked what was wrong, she made straight for the window and stared out for about ten minutes, deep in thought.

'What was it Linklater was going to move when he left your house?' she eventually asked.

'Just some information that has to be kept secret,' I replied, 'and he trusted me.'

'Cut the crap,' she snapped, 'I know what it was. It was a list, names of people to whom he circulates subversive writing. Samizdat. Tell me where he keeps this list.'

'I'm sorry darling,' I retained my air of a solicitous husband, 'I can't tell you that.'

She came towards me and clearly had difficulty containing her anger, 'So you don't trust me. You've never trusted me. You can fuck me every night, but you can't tell me one of your lousy secrets.'

'Alright, alright.' My resistance suddenly disappeared. All

those contrived arguments that sustained my stubbornness dissolved. I told her where he hid the computer disk behind a loose tile. My capitulation was so complete, so sudden, so unthinking.

Edith collapsed on the bed, as though a tremendous effort had drained all her strength. 'It's all too late now anyway,' she sighed, 'Why, Adolphus? Why didn't you tell me a few days ago? I could have got you out of this!'

The air filled with the sound of police sirens and bright artificial light beamed into our small bedroom. I could hear cars, several cars hitting their brakes outside the window, and a helicopter descending towards our building with its confusion of a deep metallic clatter and the heavy pulses of blades cutting the air. A stun grenade came crashing through the window. And just as suddenly, strong and callous arms were thrusting me to the ground and cuffing my wrists. I saw Edith being hooded and then another hood was pulled over my face. It filled up with my own stale breath, and I remember thinking that Edith had been putting up uncharacteristically little resistance. I at least had attempted to struggle, but only to discover how puny my muscles were compared with those of the men who were trussing me up with professional mastery. Thus the forces of law and order arrested two dangerous terrorists with supposed Al-Qaeda connections. By then, even I was certain of that lie, but I was to discover many more.

CHAPTER SIXTEEN

Incarceration

I RETURNED TO the CSA offices as a prisoner. After a night in the cell, I was taken into a large open-plan office to be charged. On entering, I saw a man sitting on a desk with his back to me. He had wide, uniformed shoulders and short-cropped black and grey hair. He was clearly joking or flirting with the woman who sat on the other side of the desk. As the door swung shut behind me, he turned to look at me and I immediately recognised the permanent grin and the small sunken eyes.

'Oh, so they've caught the terrorist at last,' he guffawed without a hint of self-irony.

I shuffled forward with the short humiliating steps of a man whose ankles are chained together. 'The person who said you were a police spy was right,' I said, raising my hands together as they were joined tightly by plastic cuffs. I pointed to him and said accusingly, 'Why? Why did you do it?'

His grin froze as he assessed whether to react with violence or derision. Then it became even brighter than usual. 'Police spy?' he laughed, 'we are all police spies in here, I think. It's just that some people know how to do it, and others don't.'

He looked rather proud of both the profundity and the hilarity of his statement, and the woman behind the desk seemed to share his merriment. I was charged with terrorism, consorting with terrorists, planning to plant a bomb, planting a bomb, distributing subversive material, entering Fukuyama End-Of-History Theme Parks without permission, inciting non-citizens to unlawful activities, and entering a false BB application.

The next day I was taken to see Captain Younce in an interrogation room. 'What are we going to do about you, Adolphus? You've turned out to be a great disappointment. I have been looking through your file,' he picked up a large pile of papers wrapped up in a brown folder and held together by a black ribbon, and then he let it fall back on the desk, 'and I have to say that on many occasions you have not been forthcoming with information that we really needed to know. Now, I can excuse a few peccadilloes arising from your desire to protect the girl. Very honourable of you to be so... chivalrous to the little tart. But it appears that you have also been holding back information essential to the security of the state, and in such cases I cannot be so lenient. What do you have to say for yourself?'

I was terrified. I felt sick, I was so terrified. My guts were a trembling knot and my head began to swim. I was conscious of a world closing in on me. None of the petty humiliations I had suffered since my arrest compared with the terror inspired by Captain Younce's calm and assertive coldness. 'I was confused. I couldn't understand what was going on,' I muttered.

'It was not your job to understand what was going on,' said Younce, and, raising his voice only slightly: 'Is that clear?'

'Yes.'

'That's my job,' he smiled. 'I really do not understand you, Hibbert. When I selected you, I considered you totally reliable.

As it happens, my mistake is going to cost our society a productive citizen and a BB. I know intellectuals don't know how to use liberty – convinced as they are that everyone can think exactly as they want – no, perhaps not everyone, but they definitely believe in their own inalienable right to think just as they want. This is the very reverse of loyalty, which accepts the right of someone else to decide for you. We all have to take orders from others – that is how society works. We at the CSA take our orders and execute them.'

'It seems to me that you are above the law – that you perhaps are the law,' I attempted defiance. 'It seems to me that this building is the real centre of power.'

'Then you are wrong. It is absolutely true that on certain matters government defers to us, while on others we defer to them. In a complex, highly evolved society like our own, power does not have one centre, but many. Anyway, we have no time to discuss these niceties. My point is this: you are not an intellectual; you are not like Linklater. Why do you resist?'

'I saw a former girlfriend of mine before she was probably killed in the night-club bomb.'

'Constantia. Yes, she was among the dead, I'm afraid. And that is why I appeal to you. People like you and Constantia – passive people like you are constantly victims of the activities of people like Linklater. Little people like you and Constantia are not considered in his rash and grandiose plans. That is why I find your loyalty to him so odd and misplaced.'

'He didn't have anything to do with the bomb.'

'Listen, Hibbert,' said Younce with the air of a man who running out of patience. 'I'm going to make it easy for you. If you give me a comprehensive answer to my next question, I might consider the possibility of a fairly early release. If you were to throw in a full and frank confession, I might even allow you to keep your BB, but I can't give you any guarantees. I want to know where Linklater hid the disk with the names of fellow subversives.'

'Not really subversives; it was just a mailing list for spreading a few ideas and information.'

Younce pulled a face that expressed both impatience and weariness. 'You're doing it again. You're making judgements that are not your competence. I am not interested in your definition of a subversive. My definition will do, and for the record, I considered ideas to be much more dangerous and subversive than bombs.'

'Particularly as you seem to be the one setting off the bombs.'

'Meaning?'

'I saw Nero in full CSA uniform when I was being charged.'

Younce jumped from his seat, sending his chair skidding back behind him. His face turned red with fury. I believe that he was not very practised at being angry, not because he was calm by nature, but because he was unfamiliar with contradiction or insinuation. 'I am going to let you see a friend of yours,' he shouted suppressing a sudden smile of cruel sarcasm. 'I'm sure he will be able to tell you what is in your best interest.'

He walked out of the room, indicating that I should follow. He walked at his normal brisk pace, and my manacled ankles made it hard for me to keep up with him. My absurdly short steps became painful as the metal rings chafed my lower calf muscles. He led me to another interrogation room. These rooms are all designed in the same manner: after opening a cell door which has a small liquid crystal screen displaying an image of the prisoner transmitted from a closed-circuit television camera, you enter a short corridor equipped with the various utensils required for extracting confessions; at the end of the corridor you enter the room to find a desk with the interrogator's chair closest to you. The prisoner is chained in the opposite corner, or in the case of witnesses and less serious cases, seated on the other side of the desk. Because of this, I heard the groans of the prisoner several seconds before I was able to hobble into his view.

It took me another couple of seconds before I could recognise who it was. Spartacus Linklater lay in a puddle of his own urine. His barely clad body shivered with cold and shuddered with pain. That such a gentle man could be reduced to this pitiful state was the final argument that made up my mind: I lived under a regime to which it would be immoral to make any concessions. Captain Younce clearly believed that the sight of Linklater would have a very different effect on me. 'Try speaking to him and you'll find out what happens to someone who does not co-operate with me.'

For different reasons, I did kneel down next to Linklater and, with a compassion so deep that all my own suffering seemed to melt away, I touched his bare shoulder with my two inseparable hands. 'Linklater, how are you?' I said in a slow, steady voice that did not seem my own. His only reply was a turn of the head and a sad empty expression. A river of saliva started to flow from the corner of his mouth, and I thought for a second that there was to be a flicker of a smile.

'Mr Linklater does not appear to be very talkative today,' announced Younce triumphantly. 'But I think he has told you all you need to know.' He strode off again, and I hobbled along behind him.

CHAPTER SEVENTEEN

The Interrogation

CAPTAIN YOUNCE'S SMILE was back and it was that of a man who has already won. And there can be no doubt: in one way or another he will win and I will lose. When I lie in my cell, I often tell myself that everyone has a conscience, however small or neglected. But it isn't simply a question of conscience: Younce is convinced that he is right, that he is protecting a virtuous society from malevolent forces intent upon its destruction. How much his brutality is instinctive and how much the product of his focused, all-consuming vocation for shielding credulous and vulerable citizens from the virus-like contagion of dangerous ideas, is something I will never know. He is an intelligent man and is much better versed than I whll ever be in the arguments for and against his free-market utopia. But in one sense he is my inferior: he is a fanatic, and fanaticism not only atrophies human pleasures, it impedes the proper intellectual processes of the brain. It creates will – the will to power, but in creating that will, it destroys creativity.

By the time we had returned to my interrogation room, he

must have sensed that my reaction was not exactly as he had expected. He adopted a slightly conciliatory tone. 'You may think that I overdid things with Linklater, but you have to consider the nature of the beast that we are fighting. You are by now well acquainted with the concept of history, and you will have realised that no real understanding of society is possible without it. We keep history from people to protect them, but we use it ourselves both to improve society – and I am willing to admit that there is always room for improvement – and to fight subversion, which also arms itself with history.

'In the early part of this century,' Younce continued in his newly-adopted didactic tone, 'Executor Flogg, a New York lawyer with a keen legal mind, was the first to realise that torture would have to be restored to the legal armoury. You see, torture and the death sentence were used universally until the late-eighteenth century when well-intended but very mistaken ideason personal liberties started to circulate. Italy, the same country that produced the great plutocrat Berlusconi also produced a dilettante called Beccaria who started the movement towards the abolition of torture and the death penalty. He was typical of the do-gooders whose superficially attractive ideas were to cause humanity such misery. To be fair, his ideas also led towards utilitarianism and the basic understanding that individualism and the selfish pursuit of happiness were the route to a freer and more civilised society. The utilitarians or rather some of their keener minds understood how self-interest almost mystically leads to the greatest happiness of the greatest number. Something that we can see very clearly in our society today.' He looked at me with an air of friendly condescension: 'Of course, it has its faults and some people like me have to carry out some pretty unpleasant tasks. Nobody likes hurting a poor fool like Linklater, least of all a responsible and hardworking person like myself, but I would be failing in my duty if I allowed him to get away with blatant non-cooperation with the state. Even a lean state like ours is still a state, and it has to be forthright in protecting the rules that permit free enterprise. In that sense, it's no different to a state that has a large direct involvement in the economy. We do not protect liberties in an abstract sense; we protect the one true liberty on which all other liberties depend: the liberty to act as an individual economic unit, or if you like, the liberty to succeed or fail.'

'And how do you define success and failure?' I asked.

'I know that Linklater had your RCI card removed, but damn it, Hibbert, do you have to be so predictable? And you know what my answer will be: the only real measure of success is wealth.'

'Do you really believe that?' I sneered. 'Your RCI card must be working overtime.'

'You've become very bold, Mr Hibbert. Before I show you Linklater's confession, I will therefore let you into a little secret: I have no RCI card. That's right; unlike you and Linklater, I have never been carded. You see there are various ways we recruit people. Some are frankly petty criminals, but they are mainly the lower ranks. Some, like myself, were chosen very young, before the age when our children were carded, and chosen for our academic brilliance. We were sent to finish our education at special schools. Even a state whose ideology is based on hatred of the state has to function as a state. We claim that the state has already withered away, while in reality it is a lean efficient machine. It can't be manned by carded people because it has to have an esprit de corps and a deep sense of loyalty to the state which, at the end of the day, is a collective body. I am a guardian who has been trained to defend the state ruthlessly, so my definition of success should be treated as an unbiased one. I am powerful in a way, but I am not particularly rich, so if I say that wealth is the only measure of success, I speak with humility and

I pay you a compliment.'

'So no one is carded,' I remarked. 'Not you, not myself, not Linklater, not Edith, not Foxtrotter. Everyone who plays this game is uncarded, irrespective of whether they are for carding or against it.'

'Well, the question of Edith is a little more complex,' said Younce with an ironic smile, 'but Foxtrotter has an RCI card. Of course, he has. He consumes very nicely and sells a damn good product – a totally synthetic product, I'll grant you, but a product nevertheless. Besides we live in a synthetic age in which nothing has a great deal of taste. Quantity not quality, and that applies to ideas too. The truly great ideas were all in the history age, and I love reading them. Between you and me, the Great Fukuyama was never that great, at least as a writer and thinker, but the truth he enunciated is one that I have sworn to defend, and I do so with pride. It was a truth that was staring everyone in the face: how could anyone question the fact that the West had invented the future, and that future was best encapsulated in the wonders of American democracy?'

Younce's stare was now an odd mixture of condescension, exasperation and benevolent disapproval. 'The most foolish thing you ever did,' he continued, 'was to have your Rational Consumer Implant Card removed. All you had to do was report a little information back to me in exchange for having accelerated your BB application, and then a life of wealth and leisure awaited you. Real success was in your grasp. This is why I find your behaviour so odd, and I believe your mind was not suited to decarding. Perhaps this will persuade you to play ball,' and he tossed a single sheet of rather crumpled A4 paper across his desk. Underneath the typed heading *Seventh draft of the confession of Spartacus Linklater – Prisoner SPALIN32A43X*, was the following almost illegible, hand-written note:

Having fully understood the error of my ways, I wish to confess that I headed a terrorist group that organised bomb outrages on many occasions including the recent ones in Thatcher Square and at the Popping Poppies nightclub. I attempted to incite Fukuyama people to murder carded citizens. I corrupted the minds of our young citizens and terrorised them into committing heinous acts.

It was signed underneath in poor Linklater's shaky hand. This time I felt sick not with fear but rage. 'I can see why you had to reduce him to such a state before he would write this rubbish.'

Instead of becoming angry at my insolence, Younce laughed and produced the hidden irrational guardian who lay behind the image of the committed, efficient, hardworking and rational guardian of the state. He boasted, 'Oh, he wrote that long before I had finished with him. I continued torturing him just for the fun of it! People like Linklater do not deserve an easy death.'

'Strange, because he respected you and considered you an intelligent man.'

'He said that?' came Younce's response. He seemed genuinely surprised. A fly, which had been circling the room and noisily reminding us that the well-ordered and well-scrubbed world of the CSA building was not entirely sealed off from the chaos of the natural world, flew down and attempted to land on his face. He instinctively swung his arm to rid himself of the pest and hit his nose from below, adding to his confusion and discomfort. This intelligent man had never considered Linklater's attitude towards him, so convinced he was of their mirror relationship. He must have believed that Linklater wished his death and destruction in exactly the same that he wanted Linklater's.

'Clearly the relationship was not as reciprocal as you believed,' I said with an ironic smile during the one moment of the interrogation in which I felt in a slightly stronger position.

For a moment Captain Younce looked as though his atrophied humanity might awaken and take him over, but he chased the unwelcome apparition away. 'The difference between Linklater and me is that I believe in order and he believes in disorder. People like him never give any thought to what they would replace our society with. I'll grant you that the Federation isn't perfect, but it functions, it feeds itself, it reproduces itself, it creates greater security than ever before and it provides most people with a damn good standard of living, although they don't always appreciate it.'

'And the Fukuyamas?'

'A temporary expedient,' he retorted with a wave of the hand. 'Listen, Hibbert, I would love to discuss politics with you all day, but I have a busy schedule. Are you or are you not going to tell me where the disk is, the disk with the list of fellow subversives?'

'No.'

'Who do you think you are trying to protect, Hibbert? Linklater is no more – what we saw a few minutes ago is just the useless shell of a man. Such a waste of all that erudition, don't you think? Now are you going to be a good boy, or am I going to have get tough with you?'

'You're going to have to get tough with me.'

'By God, you'll regret those words,' he shouted, but then the unwelcome apparition of his humanity must have troubled him again, because he relaxed back in his chair and quite bizarrely repeated, 'Did Linklater really say that about me? In what way did he respect me?'

I didn't answer. Younce fidgeted with items on his desk, clearly needing a few seconds to think. 'Hibbert,' he said, 'things are never as they appear. You have surprised me, but I have a bigger surprise for you: I want you to meet someone else.' He then suddenly lifted a large part of the papers in my file and brought them crashing down on the left-hand side of the interview desk.

For a moment the act seemed entirely irrational, and like all irrational acts it threatened a series of further ones. As I was attempting to determine whether his gesture was one of anger or emphasis, he lifted the papers and revealed a black object stuck underneath and surrounded by a yellow stain. Then the black object fell and it became clear that it was the troublesome fly. He stared at its corpse for a few seconds while he perhaps considered the best method for its disposal. He put the papers back in the file and then tore off two pieces of blank paper from a notepad and used the smaller one to guide the fly's crushed body onto the larger one. With a grim and nauseated expression he slowly moved the piece of paper over the wastepaper bin and then let the fly fall into it. Having been freed from the inconveniences of an instinctive violence, he looked at me in embarrassment, and I believe he was embarrassed for no other reason than his public encounter with dirt and his personal involvement with its disposal. In the meantime, the yellow stain would be archived for all eternity along with the rest of my papers. 'How the hell do they get in here?' he asked awkwardly, while he attempted to regain a physical and psychological position in which he could be more comfortable.

He called a guard and in an act of untypical generosity he had the restraints removed from my wrists and ankles. He then led me to another cell in a more gentle fashion and talked to me on the way. 'Hibbert, I want you to understand that I take no pleasure in some of the things I have to do. I am like a surgeon who has to cut out both healthy and diseased flesh in order to ensure that my patient survives. My patient is society, the body politic and a whole way of life. People take it for granted and little know that men like Captain Hieronymus Younce are working untiringly to protect them. A sense of responsibility requires thoroughness that may occasionally lead to an excess of zeal.'

We entered another interview room. Edith was sitting parallel to the table, one leg neatly on the other, her left elbow on the table surface and her left hand holding a cigarette. She wore the clothes of a citizen: a tight black acrylic pullover and a short grey skirt. She looked uncomfortable and she looked defiant.

'I'm going to leave you two little love birds on your own,' said Captain Younce with a grin. As ever he spoke in clichés, an affectation he used to increase his inscrutability. Nothing he said really seemed to belong to him. Although his words were entirely understandable, the character behind them was not. In that sense, he was the opposite of Foxtrotter. We waited for the sound of the door being shut, although we knew that it would not really increase our privacy.

While we looked at each other, I had time to realise my own monumental stupidity. I remembered that the man in the three-cornered hat had wanted to tell me something. I remembered that she had not resisted the policemen as they trussed us up. She was one of them. Which meant, of course, that I had handed over the computer disk to Younce and at that very time, the police would be picking up Linklater's network of probably fairly dormant oppositionists all over the country. It wasn't a game; it was a one-sided battle in which the powerful won before their challengers even knew what was happening.

Love, they say, is close to hate, or can become it very quickly, but I cannot say that my first reaction to Edith was one of hate. Perhaps I was feeling too guilty about my own part in the whole affair. Throughout I had been unsure whose side I was really on. Anything I did for these rebels I did for Edith and anything I did for Younce, I did out of unthinking loyalty to convention and the society in which I was brought up. I am not a natural radical and never will be, but by the time I saw Edith smoking her cigarette, I already knew clearly which side I was on. The sight of Linklater's suffering had provided the final convincing argument. The sight of her simply told me there was no way back. They knew everything already and were only interested in my obeisance. I had let the samizdat group down badly, and would never have an opportunity to put right the harm I had caused them. Perhaps Younce had continued to torture Linklater not solely out of sadism but to find out where the disk was. When he finally broke, Younce would not have been willing to give Edith any more time. Hence her change of attitude: she was no longer fighting for my survival but for hers too. My life was over, or at least my life as an independent citizen was over.

'Edith, are you a spy like Nero?' I asked, more to break the silence than in the hope of getting any reasonable reply.

She had obviously been waiting for the signal to let rip, and during her silence she had no doubt been rehearsing her arguments for what was clearly going to be an unpleasant meeting. 'That's typical of you citizens. You think you can sit there in judgement over us. You know nothing of our lives. You have always had everything. What do you know about not being able to buy decent clothes, decent furniture, decent kitchenware, a decent lifestyle? You think you can sit there …'

'Not everyone in the Fukuyamas is a police spy.'

'Plenty are, plenty are,' she spat.

'And plenty are not. Although I would never have imagined it, I think some have more interesting and productive lives than we citizens do.'

'Oh aren't we the liberal, these days? You'll start speaking like Linklater next. Have you any idea about what it was like being brought up by my mother, the Mass as they call her?'

I could see that she had been around citizens for some time, because she had adopted the common habit amongst them of blaming all their troubles on their parents. On the other hand, I have to admit that being brought up by the Mass could not have been as much fun as being brought up by the musician's all-singing, all-dancing, all-playing parents with their friends, their stories and their languages. I still couldn't find it in me to be angry with Edith, but on the other hand I wasn't going to pass up the opportunity for an interrogation of my own.

'Why did you insist on my not giving you away, if you were the other spy? Why did you appeal to my loyalty to you? A loyalty that I took seriously.'

'I'm sorry, Adolphus,' she whispered, staring at her feet. 'I entered my own fantasy and made it reality.' She looked up at me, and the bold, defiant Edith re-emerged. 'You'll find this difficult to believe, but I did care about you. Some of the time, I really felt I was a subversive and not a government spy. I thought I could save us both and get my citizenship too.'

'The secret of good lying is to believe one's own lies,' I said sententiously. 'I too thought I could save us both,' and I told her of my plans for an idyllic life beyond the boundaries of the Western world. 'I was willing to sacrifice not only my wealth and BB, but also the citizenship that you care so much about.'

'Oh, sure,' she replied heatedly, 'take the moral high ground. What do you know about growing up in a smelly Fukuyama? Linklater thinks that all Fukuyama people, indeed all uncarded people, are saints – all brotherly love and mutual assistance. There is undoubtedly an element of solidarity in the Fukuyamas, but there is also competition, envy and brutal, pointless malice. He should have known that, with all the history he was constantly studying.'

'Intellectuals, I now believe, will always prefer their own ideas, their generalisations, in place of what they are told by reality. Linklater wishes to believe that all humans are basically good, and Younce wishes to believe they're all fundamentally bad and need to be moulded by a strong paternal hand.'

'Well, whatever,' she retorted, 'the fact is that Fukuyama people can be cruel, and they were cruel to my mother. You know, she was repeatedly and brutally raped by a BB; sometimes it was just him, sometimes he brought his friends. No one, but no one, did anything to help her. Everyone knew what was going on. Perhaps you could excuse them because of their fear of the authorities, but once it stopped, did they show any solidarity to my mother? Or to me, the product of those savage unions? We were ostracised, and my mother neglected herself. She put on weight and refused to speak except when absolutely necessary.'

'I did notice that she is a woman of few words.'

'Oh really,' said Edith cuttingly, 'of few words! The "Mass" they call her. Little do they know she is a mass of words. She is an Abkhazian Christian. Abkhazia is a little country within the little country of Georgia, which was once part of the Soviet Union and before that the Tsarist Empire. Her culture was rooted in an Abkhazian, Georgian and Russian past. Not only was she from a minority within a minority, she was from a religious minority within that minority, because Abkhazia was predominantly Muslim. That's why she came to England. That's why so many Chechens also came, because they were a Muslim people in predominantly Christian Russia. You see, I agree with Captain Younce when he says the masses cannot be trusted with real democracy. My mother's people had lived in that corner of the globe under undemocratic empires for centuries, and nobody hurt them too much as long as they worked hard and paid their taxes. Then the ideologies and fanatical religions of the twentieth century came along, and peoples all round the world were destroyed. Captain Younce says that humans can only be trusted with their own greed, and perhaps he is right.'

'I'm sorry Edith. I didn't realise that you and your mother suffered so much. But you mustn't lose faith in people. Younce is wrong: people are not a mass, people are individuals.'

'People are a great mass,' said Edith assertively, 'against which you have to struggle alone if you are not to be suffocated beneath them. My mother never displayed anything other than gentleness. She never complained, and I only found out about my cursed origins from others. She never expected anything of life, and she was certainly never given anything. I was determined never to be like her – to fight my way up the greasy pole.' Then she added in a bitter and more subdued voice, 'Maybe I just take after my bastard father.'

'Edith, I was in love with you. I was never in love before. I am unlikely to be in love again, as I doubt they'll ever let me out of here – that is one of the many things I realised when I saw you sitting there in your citizen's clothes. Perhaps the Rational Consumer Implant Card is not such a bad idea after all: my short uncarded experience has produced emotions I find too difficult to assess. I don't know whether my love for you was a stupid, shallow emotion based on some irrational and animal instinct, or a fine altruism that has dignified my existence.'

'Oh shit,' said Edith, and then did something I really hadn't expected: she started to cry. 'Oh shit, I did think of telling you. I did. I promise. Younce knew that I was feeling the strain; that's why he finally promised to release me from my duties after he got the disk, and let me become a citizen.' She wiped her tears first with the pulse of one hand and then with the other, sniffed heavily and lifted her head to look at me with a half-smile and a half tearful grimace. 'Perhaps it was both.'

'Perhaps what was both?'

'Perhaps your love for me was both something fine and something shallow. I can speak as someone who has long experience of being uncarded: every emotion carries experience of its opposite, and every certainty is accompanied by an equally intense doubt. Uncarded life is about building barriers between these experiences, and if successful, life can be quite good. My short experience of being carded is like the cloud of an antidepressant: I don't feel bad, but simply empty of any drive.'

'So you've had the operation. Of course you have. You're a citizen now.' And then with a trace of sarcasm, I added, 'It always seemed to me that you would make the perfect consumer.'

'That's a lie, Adolphus; you thought I was an exciting subversive. And I was a rebel, once. That's why I failed the first integration tests to become a citizen after leaving school – if you can call those places schools. Many of my friends went but I just told the panel where they could put their citizenship. Then I had a relationship with a BB who came down to listen to the music at the Ticket Office. He bought me lots of presents and I suppose I developed tastes that couldn't be satisfied in a Fukuyama, at least not after he dumped me. Shortly afterwards, Younce appeared and offered me work. Then the bastard said I was too good to be made a citizen, and he kept me there for years, always giving me more money and property but never fulfilling his promise to make me a citizen. But now I see how right Linklater was: pleasure is more in the anticipation than in the attainment.'

'Maybe life will be very dull, now that you've got what you wanted.'

'Maybe. Maybe you're right,' she said in a sad voice that seemed to confirm the remark I had actually made in a spirit of hopeless spite. Her vulnerability touched me deeply. It was as though a lifetime of emotions were to be played out within the walls of this prison after so much of my life had been deprived of all sensitivity. 'I was mad with Younce for not making me a citizen,' Edith went on, 'but in a way that ambition structured my life. And I was always improving my own situation. I had two houses in two different Fukuyamas, and I was somebody in each of them, because I had more money than most of the inmates put together – although Younce said I shouldn't throw my money around too much or I would attract attention and ruin my usefulness as a spy. And now I'm a citizen, I can't visit either of my homes, and they've put me on a ghastly estate where they integrate Fukuyama people. It's not at all what I was expecting. It's so tacky.'

Listening to my Edith speak, I could feel my love for her begin to fade. Even now, this was not something I wanted to happen. I struggled to believe our love was something sacred that could survive our being placed on different sides, more by circumstance than choice. Then she produced another surprise: she leapt from her chair, threw her arms around my neck and breathed the words, 'But I loved you too.' Anger took hold and I pushed her away.

'At least, I think I did,' she said in a low sulking voice. 'It's impossible to remember anything now. Impossible to grasp any feeling or thought. More particularly, it is impossible to care.'

'Listen,' I cried in an agitated voice as I now paced around the room. 'They'll want a confession from me. I'm in this right up to my neck. I told them things I shouldn't have told them precisely because I imagined you being tortured in some other cell. They showed me Linklater and I knew you had been wrong about him, but I still believed in you. They'll want a confession and if I don't say exactly what they want, they'll torture me.'

'Then say what they want.'

'I don't know that I can.'

'What do you mean? You never really believed in any of that stuff.'

'Well, I wasn't sure of anything, but now I am.'

She looked shocked. 'You can't be. You wanted to be a BB, for Christ's sake.'

'Look I'm a coward. I would like someone to take this from me. I would like to walk out of here and return to my old life. But I know that is no longer possible, partly because they simply won't let me and partly because my mind can never unlearn the things I have learnt in the last six months. You might not understand that, but they do. That's why they will always keep me in here or another place like here.'

She then said something I will always treasure, or rather will treasure as long as they leave me a glimmer of sanity. It is much more important to me than the declaration of love she made just before, whose sincerity and endurance have to be questioned. She said, 'the only truly courageous men are cowards'. Those words, those dear words affected me not really because of their truth – I am not even convinced they have any – but because with them Edith, through the fog of her newly acquired RCI card, left her anguish and her desires behind, and judged me from that objective place that hides in the depth of our souls, and she did not find me wanting. She got up and walked slowly across the room. She did not touch me, but only said quietly, 'Adolphus, make love to me here. Make love to me for the last time. What does it matter about the rest of time, about them, about our own stupid miserable lives? We have this moment. That is all we have.'

I then did something inexplicable. Without kissing my love one last time, without feeling the cool softness of her skin, without saying that I understood that neither of us had had any real power in this stupid game, I went to the door and knocked on it. Captain Younce reappeared almost immediately and took me away. I did not even turn to look at Edith, and I believe that was the most pointlessly cruel act I committed in my life. Maybe I was enjoying some foolish sense of moral superiority. Perhaps some small display of affection would have given our parting a different and possibly better meaning, but the idea of making love in a Spartan interview room which was undoubtedly stuffed with listening devices and hidden cameras was not the most attractive. In any case, the offer was almost certainly made in the certainty of its refusal. What it asked of me, and this was the further dishonesty, was an act of forgiveness, possibly confirmed by a minimal act of affection. Had I become so moralistic, so intoxicated with my sense of sacrifice that I was unable to concede her that? It would have cost me nothing. On the other hand, my actions might have been an unintended kindness. She might have been acting not out of love but guilt, or more likely a mixture of both. The love and the guilt sustained each other, and so by turning my back on her, I have kept her love alive. If we had made love on that cold floor or even if I had simply expressed my forgiveness, she might have felt that some debt had been paid, and then she could forget me in the struggle and miserable squalor of her new life (seemingly less squalid than before but actually more so because of her relative position to others and because she would lack the Fukuyama's human solidarity which generates a special human dignity). Because I turned my back on her, she will always think of me and my sacrifice, and, at the risk of the reader taking me for a complete romantic (and he will because he is some obtuse policeman), I believe that the thought of my sacrifice will lighten her life. Whatever she suffers, she will think of me and that suffering will go. They can stick RCI cards in people's brains, but I am sure that these things only really work if you let them, if you let that part of you which has always been there take over your brain. However much they play around with the fabric of our physical selves, they can never really destroy what I will call the soul, because I cannot think of any other word and this one seems to make sense. They can suffocate it or we can neglect it, but it remains stubbornly there. That's perhaps why I turned my back on her: there was nothing more to add or do to our relationship. I'm sure she knows that I do not hate her; I hope she knows that something of my love for her remains. And my love is not a purely sexual one; it is perhaps no longer a sexual one. My love for Edith is a love for the beautifully compromised nature of human life. Her selfishness was never arrogant, and her ignorance was never stupid. Her emotions were never pure, not because of any failure inherent to them, as in carded people, but because they always had to be tempered by a need to survive. Perhaps the End-of-History has robbed us of the need to survive and therefore the need for justifiable compromise. It is compromise that makes us desire purity. We detest compromise and paradoxically that detestation partially purifies us. Remove the need for enforced compromise and you remove the desire for purity: everything turns to mud.

I had never met anyone like Edith, and I believe that the history period was full of Ediths struggling to survive but not struggling too hard. That is the terrible problem with the End-of-History: life is too easy here and too hard in the Third World. The balanced existence represented by Edith is now a rarity. Or do I simplify and romanticise a past I never knew and can never know? History, I think, has two salutary functions: it helps us understand who we are, and it defies understanding. I am in danger of forgetting that latter function, because I am a newcomer to it; Linklater never made that kind of mistake.

CHAPTER EIGHTEEN

Explanations and Justifications

LINKLATER USED TO tell me that religions also have two functions: the ethical and the salvationist. As religions got older, the ethical dimension became less important and the salvationist more important. Ethics, he said, is concerned with how we behave in this world and salvationism with what will happen in the next, about which we can know nothing and on which it is foolish to speculate. He was only interested in this next world in as much as it too affects human behaviour here on earth. At the beginning of what he called the Modern Era, Christianity had almost entirely lost its ethical dimension and the salvationist dimension had taken it to the heights of absurdity. Society started to secularise and the secularists reinvented ethics in the form of the Enlightenment, further driving religion into its own salvationist ghetto. At the turn of the century, there was a very good example of this, at least according to Linklater. The American president George Bush called himself a Christian, but he was constantly throwing the first stone and executing criminals, often on very slim evidence. He was constantly judging who was 'good' and who was 'evil' when he should have remembered that he who judges will be judged. He terrorised countries in a war on terror which was little more than a war against another religion, and he believed in the righteousness of wealth, forgetting Christ had believed in the righteousness of poverty. To give an example of how things had changed, Linklater told me about a powerful emperor called Charlemagne who had executed four thousand Saxon rebels. For this act he was fiercely criticised by church leaders and told not to force conversions in his future wars. Early Islam too was careful to avoid forced conversion and respected other peoples' religions.

At the same time that this Bush character was twisting his religion into salvationist intolerance, he also claimed to be in the tradition of an American revolutionary and Enlightenment figure called Jefferson who believed it was wrong to concentrate too much wealth in too few hands. Linklater taught me these things and told me they were paradoxical. When I asked him why, he said that no country had been so clearly founded on the principles of Christianity and the Enlightenment as the United States of America, and by the time of Bush no country had become so entirely bereft of them both. 'They respected neither Christ nor Beccaria.'

Closed in this cell, I can sense that we now live not at the end of history, but at the end of human compassion and ethical ideas. Whatever moves the heavy footsteps in the corridors, the shouted commands and the busy business of holding a state together, it is not based on any ethical imperative, however distorted by the inevitable logic of power. It is not even the case of the ends justifying the means: now the end belongs to the past, we have neither means nor ends, but simply the justification of all acts through the absolute present.

I now think that if I were to mix Linklater's ideas with those of the man in the three-cornered hat – the guarded optimism of the former with the justifiable pessimism of the latter – then I could get somewhere near the truth. I have finally understood what I would like to do with my life: I would like to devote it to marrying those contradictory currents together, but I have no time and I have no skills. Not that I believe you need to be a particularly special man or woman to understand these things, but you do need special circumstances: a society affluent enough to provide the basics of existence and a society educated enough to listen and understand.

In all these matters, we constantly come back to time and our increasingly efficient use of it. Since I got caught up in words, ideas and terrible events, it has always struck me that in a society that has finally created mass leisure, we are unable to create our own cultural products, but have to steal them unaltered from previous ages – 'from history', as we like to say. We are incapable of speaking to our own time and, I believe, all the reasons for this relate to our abuse of time. Firstly, we have banned time by banning history, and that means we have no idea of who we are. I understand what Younce is getting at when he says that popular history is full of dangerous myths, and I can even grudgingly admit that the deluded Foxtrotter was not entirely wrong when he implied that not everyone can gain deep historical insights, but where there is a spirit of tolerance surely some historical memory is required to hold society together. Secondly, by banning time we live our lives within an apparently unchanging present. Everyone in our society is an ideal twenty-to-thirty-year-old. Even when we are forty or fifty, we live as though we were still young and were going to live forever. The greater the probability of living into old age, the greater our fear of not doing so. Thirdly, we have emptied leisure time of any useful purpose by making it an economic activity; it is now all about consumption and the GDP, and no longer about creativity, reflection, quiet, conversation, music-making and the joy of being human beings temporarily released from the business of providing for ourselves, however pleasant or unpleasant that other activity might be.

Prison gives you time to reflect on time, because here there is an abundance of it punctuated by sudden flurries of action, none of them agreeable. In the end you get to prefer inaction and time as a chasm into which you have been suspended – time as an inability to act. After leaving Edith, I spent a long period in my cell. Days, but I am not sure how many. Then suddenly the door swung open and in marched Captain Younce. He sat down at the desk and no one pushed me onto the other chair or tied me to it. He signalled that I should sit down and then looked at me much as a headmaster might look at a difficult pupil for whom he has some inexplicable affinity, or even affection. 'There is,' he said, 'little else you could possibly need to know. You now know who Linklater was and who Edith was. You now know their respective fates, and you must have a good idea as to what yours will be. I want to make it easy for you, Adolphus. I want to help you.'

He took out a fountain pen and placed a sheet of paper on top of my file. It had a printed paragraph at the top, and below it he started to write copious notes. Eventually, he looked up quickly with that busy, time-efficient smirk of his – a concession to good manners. 'I know what you're thinking, Adolphus. You're thinking that we let off bombs and blame them on terrorists, and that shocks you. That is understandable, even commendable. It does you a lot of credit. You've learnt a little history in the last few months, so I'm going to give you a history lesson of my own.

'When the forerunner countries of the Federation finally defeated the communist colossus in 1991, they realised that that defeat had not been in their long-term interests. We interpret life as though it were a novel or a story. The hero has his revenge, gets his girl and discovers his treasure, or in tragic mode he dies as the human sacrifice to Justice Reaffirmed. But in the real world, those who do not die live on to experience the repeated tragedy, comedy and sheer banality of life. Let me just add that banality should be the undeclared aim of any sensible and responsible state. In many languages, they use the same word for 'end' and 'aim', and so do we to some extent, although as the practical people we are, 'end' in this sense retains a certain unreliable foreign-ness. Our founding fathers realised that aims should never be fully achieved as their achievement leaves a vacuum, incurs terrible *restructuring* costs, and introduces a dangerous element: the uncertainty of certainty and the inconclusiveness of finality. The principal end has undoubtedly been achieved, but its consolidation depends on a few loose ends remaining unresolved. This is the sublime, one might say sacred, revelation of End-of-History theory: it is the key to human happiness. What Fukuyama failed to comprehend fully is that the End-of-History is not heaven's gift in perpetuity; having been won, it has to be defended. My job is to defend the End-of-History, and I am part of a team of guardians who devote their lives in different ways to this difficult and sensitive task.

'Now how do we, as a state, go about protecting the End-of-History?' he asked rhetorically, and his eyes smiled professorially over a pair of half-glasses I had never seen him wear before. 'We protect the values of our state, which is a kind of enlightened suspended animation, by taking the fight to them, and by "them" I mean the Muslims and other Third-Worldists. We invade their countries, shatter their borders and disrupt their trade, but we never completely defeat them and we never stay on after we have wreaked destruction – that was our mistake in Iraq in the early part of this century.'

Again his eyes smiled and his mouth attempted to follow their lead. He took my silence to be acquiescence, while in fact I was past persuasion. I felt somewhere in my feeble brain a doubt – a doubt that wanted to become a prophecy: could it be that this policy was no defence at all, but merely put off the final reckoning which would be all the more terrible the later it came. He smiled again with the nearest thing to friendship that can exist in the mind of a man who holds another entirely in his power. In as much as it was friendship, it was genuine friendship because he could not hate me as he had hated Linklater; I was not important enough for such passion. I also represented a means for him to exorcise any minor sense of guilt he felt over the way he had treated his rival, because very few powerful men ever feel that they are wicked or even slightly lax about morality, and they overcome any problems of conscience by attempting to cover up their great acts of evil with small acts of good; they always succeed.

He was willing to make a few concessions. 'Of course, we make a few mistakes but we are learning all the time: the longer the system is in place, the more firmly established it becomes. I feel more confident today that we have truly embarked on the End-of-History than I did when I started my career. In that sense, I feel that my life's work has been a success and, Adolphus, I would ask you – beg you – not to throw your life away on a hopeless cause. Co-operate and I promise to work on your behalf. Once we are confident of your reliability as a citizen and consumer, we could return you to liberty. Who knows,' he added unconvincingly, 'we might even return your Berlusconi Bonus.' And then he contradicted claims he had made at a previous meeting. 'We can do anything. Believe me: all real power is here! The heart of the Lean State is a powerful and hidden reality; it is a machine of tempered steel that quietly and efficiently pumps the lifeblood of what is, at the end of the day, a soft, pampered and, let's be honest, rather thoughtless society. In return for our dedication and sacrifice, the citizens of the Federation of Free Democratic States have delegated all power – all sovereignty –

to us, the guardians. No fair-minded person could either object or fail to see the common sense in that.'

I had no doubts about the extent of his power, but I did about the reliability of his promises. He may have been sincere at the time, but the weeks, let alone the years, would almost certainly diminish his commitment to a prisoner of little importance. There was no way back, so considerations of regret were pointless. However, my intellectual curiosity had been sufficiently aroused for me to ask myself whether I would have abandoned this bitter cup, had a genuine opportunity arisen to return to my former state of freedom and privilege. Even now, as I write these suicidal notes, I think I would definitely choose freedom if offered a real chance. If I could get back out there, I would not fight Linklater's hopeless fight; I would hide myself away with books and continue his intellectual work without involvement. This is not a time for change. This is not a time for hope. They are out of season. Linklater should just have observed and kept a record to be discovered by later historians – a record of a terrible age entirely lacking in self-awareness. I remember him telling me that Fukuyama claimed that the End-of-History was the achievement of a state of absolute self-consciousness, and then chuckling at the idea of this state being embodied by Fukuyama, George Bush and Donald Rumsfeld. I cannot imagine a state of absolute self-consciousness, which must surely be the prerogative of gods. Men are gifted with doubts – their greatest asset. And those doubts might provide them with some kind of relative self-consciousness.

Captain Younce added to the air of a social meeting between friends by lighting up a cheroot. 'Smoking,' he said in a relaxed voice, 'is a very irrational act, but a complete godsend to a chap who doesn't have an RCI card stuck in his head.' He lay back in his chair and exhaled a cloud of smoke towards the ceiling as if to prove what fun it was. 'It is so expensive, and these ones are made of the finest tobacco. Everyone needs a little vice, but don't think that I don't look after my health,' he added as though he believed I was genuinely concerned. 'I go running everyday and regularly attend the "well-man's clinic" here in this building. Remember, Adolphus, a healthy mind in a healthy body – that's what the ancients said. Very good advice, particularly for a busy guardian like myself.' I will never know whether there was any intended irony in this advice to a man condemned to the unhealthy life of prison and possible torture.

I expect that the elimination of Spartacus Linklater was a big moment in Captain Younce's career. He had not hurried it, and the eventual denouement brought its inevitable satisfactions. Hence his relative expansiveness. As though remembering an unforgivable oversight, he suddenly rummaged in the inside pocket of his jacket and produced his silver box of cheroots. 'I'm terribly sorry! Would you like one too?' he asked as he extended his hand and triggered the spring mechanism of the lid to reveal a set of three cheroots neatly held to a silk lining by a decorated elastic ribbon. It also revealed something about Captain Younce's fastidious nature and old-fashioned love of the intricate and expertly crafted – in other words, of the things that are not generally available in our consumer paradise. 'You're uncarded, so you will probably appreciate a good smoke. You know,' he paused to puff appreciatively on his cheroot, 'studies have shown us that fifty per cent of BBs have had their cards removed. Do we care? Of course not. Their influence on the economy as consumers is statistically irrelevant.'

I was still looking at the cheroots, undecided whether or not to accept. Acceptance would mean establishing a bond between us. It would have been foolish to alienate him, and it looked as though my life was not going to offer me many more physical experiences. I took one without saying anything, but smiled at him by way of thanks. Captain Younce was such an Englishman

– at least of the boarding-school kind. He was a piece of history himself. And yet he worked untiringly for the Americanisation of the little province in which he was born. Soon there would be no more men like Captain Younce and the shiny corridors of the CSA building would resound to another more homogenised and less quirky culture. These future, rootless guardians might be even worse than the current ones.

'Good man, Adolphus,' he grinned and puffed on his own cheroot again. 'Good man. Cuban, you know.' He puffed again and swivelled his chair so that he was no longer facing directly towards me. 'What was she like?' he asked conspiratorially.

'Who?' I said stupidly. I studied the cheroot carefully. It was beautifully made, slightly knobbly like a twig and a product of nature, but also smooth, symmetrical and delicate like the manufactured good it was. A perfectly trimmed outer leaf wrapped up the compact contents in a dense promise of refined physical pleasure. I put it in my mouth inexpertly.

'The little Fukuyama tart, of course,' he said as he held out a lighter and ignited its flame. I realised then that the camaraderie of small cigars required derogatory talk about women. With my first puff I exploded into a fit of coughing, and this triggered Younce's equally violent explosion into a fit of laughter. I was aware of an idiotic and unpleasant ritual which only underscored my helplessness and strengthened my resolve to defy Younce. He stood up and came round the desk to give me a hearty slap on the back.

'Good man, Adolphus,' he condescended, 'good sport, damn good sport!' I played the part and smiled at him while my throat burned and my eyes watered. 'No time and you'll be back at the BB Club. And now I've initiated you to the superb taste of these Cubans, you'll be able to hand them around. They'll go down very well. Actually it's a BB who supplies them to me. We poor government servants can't afford such things,' he displayed another of his absurd conceits.

'You can promise me that?' I asked bluntly.

'Adolphus, I cannot promise you anything other than my own goodwill.'

'I thought you had so much power.'

'I said that the CSA is the ultimate seat of power, or at least I implied it, because these are not things we generally talk about. We still like to call ourselves a democracy, but frankly...'

He appeared to have forgotten about his desire to discuss Edith, and besides there is a kind of rhetoric in those questions. They do not require an honest answer. He had recalled the real purpose of our meeting: he turned his chair back towards me and stared me in the eyes with his own cold, penetrating pupils. 'You are going to have to write a confession; you understand that? Normally it would have to be detailed and penitent.' Then he just as quickly returned to his former amiable self: he swung his chair back through forty-five degrees, and leaning back with his cigar hand raised high, he said, 'Just a formality, Adolphus. In your case, it does not have to be too long or too detailed. Normally information is even more important than contrition, but I already know everything there is to know about this case. So, contrition, young man! That's the thing that will keep me and, more importantly, my superiors happy. Because we all have superiors, Adolphus. You understand? We all have superiors, and none of us are indispensable. Although we do, of course, like to think so.' He smiled happily and graciously. 'Adolphus, we always leave our suspects in peace when they are writing their confessions, or at least their first confession. In your case, Adolphus, I am willing to grant you Grade One comfort, which means a cell-flat with kitchen, a small collection of books and a decent computer with printer. After all, you are or were a BB, and deserve a little consideration. Just a formality, I repeat. Take your time, be contrite and who knows what will come out of it.'

But I have decided to defy him by writing not a confession but a precise account of the events up to and including my imprisonment. And I write this account in part to clarify my own ideas before Younce destroys my mind, just as he destroyed Linklater's much finer one. I write to lay before him an accusation of abuse of power and of needless cruelty. I hold these pages up to him as a mirror, and am willing to face his wrath. I hope this is an act of defiance and not folly or even masochistic delusion – it is definitely not an act of heroism. My treatment would not alter greatly in return for my obeisance, and that small difference would not justify allowing Captain Younce to think better of himself. When he discovers that these notes are not a confession but an impassioned *J'accuse*, I will ruin his morning. That is the only kind of victory that the powerless can ever achieve over the powerful: the ruination of a morning or some other minor discomfort. It does not take a genius to perceive the evils of this state, and yet few take notice. Such is the mesmeric effect of great power. Those who criticise the state are treated with contempt and tainted with anti-Federationism, which is somehow considered a very childish and ineffectual state of mind, even when it is adorned with endless qualifications and caveats. On the other hand, unadorned scorn for Islam, the EU, Fukuyama people and any country in the Third World is considered not only good sense, but 'almost a patriotic duty and, in a man, a sign of virility. But none of this detracts from the basic truth of the main accusations against this society: its wastefulness, its deep discontents, its oppression of the rest of the world, its destruction of our planet and its resulting instability.

A truth that is continually repeated becomes a banality, but it is still no less of a truth. Truths are generally repeated because many people, any people who leave behind their prejudices, their cherished myths and their national prides, will know that we are doing wrong and doing things wrong. These lightning wars bring us no benefit, unless a chauvinist pleasure in power over the weak can count as a benefit. These denials of our human nature and the variety of our human natures can bring us no benefit, unless a mindless, sedated consumer binge can be counted as a benefit. This refusal to engage in open democratic debate in search of complex, difficult and often not wholly satisfactory solutions brings us no benefit, unless ignorance and parrot-like credos can be counted as a benefit.

Nothing beautiful or good is permanently won. It has to be laboriously re-buttressed and readapted in every generation. This requires peace, intelligence and goodwill. We have peace, because we have exported war, but no society founded solely on the satisfaction of material desires can be intelligent, and sadly goodwill is often generated by terrible events and not by the immense security we have been taught to feel. We take for granted the social goods that surround us and we ignore how they are constantly undermined by the powerful. That makes us better than these ugly *thymotic* thugs, but not much better. Our silence condemns us.

Those philosophers who believe that they have discovered the key to unlock history and stop the mechanisms that drive it, not forward but in a circular clock-like motion, are not mistaken in thinking that human history will come to an end. They are mistaken, however, in thinking that it will be anything more complicated than the end of human life on this planet. In this, *homo sapiens* is no different from the humble dodo.

Fukuyama's metaphor of history as a wagon train on the way to the town where history can cease is both absurd and telling. Absurd because there is no destination, and telling because the directionless route of the free-market economy always drives through other people's lands sowing destruction in its endless desire for stuff, the mixtures of molecules that nature and geological happenchance have hidden like so many treasures around the globe for the children of plenty to find. The American Indians who attack the wagon-train are presumably excluded from humanity's great journey. Perhaps Fukuyama's model needs exclusions, and that is why the Native Americans, now reduced to insignificant numbers, have been replaced by Muslims, who are barred by their supposedly perfidious religion from the joining the glorious cavalcade towards Sales and Loans City on the other side of the prairie strewn with perished social systems. These systems failed because they were unable to compete with the good folks in the wagons who stare unflinchingly at the featureless horizon of hope and hold their store catalogues firmly in their hand like bibles.

But in whom can we place our hopes if even such gentle selfless souls as Linklater have their flaws? I have an image of him fixed in my mind, alongside the more recent and harrowing one. It is of his lanky figure bending towards me after he had admitted that he had no proof that the man with the three-cornered hat was an informer. He lifted his index finger to his temple and twisted it slightly to indicate that in any case he doubted the man's sanity. Now I know the rationalism of one and the rationalism of the other, now that I respect them both, I realise that Linklater could not listen to the Fukuyama people because he wanted to help them as a people, and therefore had to idealise them and perceive them as a uniform mass of righteousness. The man with the three-cornered hat challenged that belief and was therefore suspect. If devoted to a cause, even a gentle and tolerant man can have his areas of blindness and deafness, because he is interested not in what is but in what should be. Of course, Linklater would have denied this. He was aware of the problem of utopias; my point is that the danger is there even with someone who is sensitive to the risks, because the minute we move beyond our selfishness towards some kind of universal awareness or love, we turn into moral animals who think in categories, and if we fall back to earth clinging to our universal love as a badge of honour, then we become moralistic animals – the worst sort. In conceding this, I do not concede the argument to the utilitarian exponents of enlightened self-interest, I merely point to the paradoxical tragedy of those who justly stand up to them. The flaw does not detract from Linklater's tragic ending; it adds to it.

The sadness I feel at Linklater's destruction knows no finite end, no depth that touches bottom and brings, if not relief, at least the sense that nothing worse can happen or be felt. Forget that I finally came to consider him a friend, a dear and admirable friend, perhaps only after I last saw him sane. Forget that he taught me to be aware of the world we live in, and brought some meaning to a life whose meaninglessness I had not been aware of previously. Forget that because I knew him, I now perceive the world in much brighter colours – the colours of a world that has a before and an after. Forget that he always displayed great selflessness, wisdom and above all gentleness. At every turn, at every moment I think of him, there opens up another abyss of sorrow – a great potential for human wastefulness. I thought, for instance, that as he dies, somewhere here amongst the malls and gated communities of our land, a more violent enemy is being formed in the shape of the propaganda stereotypes invented by Captain Younce: a man who will not propagate Linklater's egalitarianism based on love, but a much cruder and more extreme one based on hate. I do not believe that this man – for he will be a man – will be born among the dispossessed, the many dispossessed of this earth. No, he will be among the privileged of this earth, a man who, driven by a real or imagined slight, girds his armour of outrage – and there is reason enough for outrage – to vindicate himself and his self-image, and imposes his rigid morality on all through a harsh and puritanical will to power. He will unleash not only the justifiable anger of the oppressed but will mould them into hysterical madmen intent on unending revenge. Linklater told me of twentieth-century leaders who took up just causes and exploited the resulting power of hysteria to build labour camps and pursue the perfect man by murdering all those they considered imperfect.

I believe that with Linklater's death the way has been closed off to the power of gentleness, and the way has been opened to the power of hate. Humanity sinks back to an even lower level, and one day the power of hate will destroy this entire consumer paradise and replace it with a brutally Spartan one. There will be a personality cult – the cult of a mediocre mind above which no other mind will be allowed to rise – and so this absurd ideological pendulum will continue, with its absolute models, its mythologies, its subject lifestyles and above all its secret services – the guardians who protect the absolute while they alone are allowed to think.

[The printout then contains a handwritten note from Captain Younce, 'This is not a confession. It is an abomination and an insult to the guardians. Have Adolphus Hibbert tortured and his second draft confession on my desk before the week is out – H Younce.']

Some other books published by **Luath** Press

The Golden Menagerie
Allan Cameron
1 84282 057 5 PBK £9.99

For Lucian Heatherington-Jones, a pink-haired, punk adolescent from Croydon, his meeting with a mirth-seeking sect plunges him into a series of nightmarish metamorphoses from which he can only be saved by the wise and magnanimous (and beautiful) Fotis. Drawing on themes from ancient mythology, eschewing the expected and thoroughly engaging the reader, *The Golden Menagerie* stylishly defies our concept of the novel – and entertains.

Allan Cameron writes beautifully, sometimes with easy economy, at other times with a startling sharp pinprick of humour.
ALISTAIR MOFFAT

… fantastic invention and reflections on the human predicament… consistently fascinating and readable, the work of a writer of high intelligence who has a stylish way with words.
ERIC HOBSBAWM, historian

… a humorous, wild… critique of the human state… This is a beautiful tale… highly rewarding, in the richness, precision and hmour of its language…
SCOTTISH REVIEW OF BOOKS

Luath Press Limited

committed to publishing well written books worth reading

LUATH PRESS takes its name from Robert Burns, whose little collie Luath (*Gael.*, swift or nimble) tripped up Jean Armour at a wedding and gave him the chance to speak to the woman who was to be his wife and the abiding love of his life. Burns called one of *The Twa Dogs* Luath after Cuchullin's hunting dog in *Ossian's Fingal.* Luath Press was established in 1981 in the heart of Burns country, and is now based a few steps up the road from Burns' first lodgings on Edinburgh's Royal Mile. Luath offers you distinctive writing with a hint of unexpected pleasures.

Most bookshops in the UK, the US, Canada, Australia, New Zealand and parts of Europe, either carry our books in stock or can order them for you. To order direct from us, please send a £sterling cheque, postal order, international money order or your credit card details (number, address of cardholder and expiry date) to us at the address below. Please add post and packing as follows: UK – £1.00 per delivery address; overseas surface mail – £2.50 per delivery address; overseas airmail – £3.50 for the first book to each delivery address, plus £1.00 for each additional book by airmail to the same address. If your order is a gift, we will happily enclose your card or message at no extra charge.

Luath Press Limited
543/2 Castlehill
The Royal Mile
Edinburgh EH1 2ND
Scotland
Telephone: 0131 225 4326 (24 hours)
Fax: 0131 225 4324
email: gavin.macdougall@luath. co.uk
Website: www. luath.co.uk